In Desperate Straits

In Desperate Straits

By

CARRIE FANCETT PAGELS

Hearts Overcoming Press

Mackinac Island Romances Series - Prequel

ISBN: 978-1-7366875-7-4

©2019, Second Revised Edition 2024 Carrie Fancett Pagels

Cover Design: Hearts Overcoming Press
Model Image: Shutterstock

Hearts Overcoming Press
Published in the USA

Dedication

To Mary Jane Barnwell & Tamara Tomac for sharing and encouraging the love of Mackinac Island books at the Island Bookstore and for their many kindnesses toward me.

Characters List

Margaret "Maggie" AKA Mickey Hadley - daughter of owners of Hadley Percherons Farm

       Buck Hadley, Maggie's father

              Russell & John Hadley – older brothers

Jesse Calhoun Huntington – Recent college graduate, son of a wealthy Charleson family

       (Rutherford Huntington – Jesse's father, deceased)

       Camille Calhoun Huntington – Jesse's Mother

              Vivienne "Vivie" Huntington – Jesse's sister

              Florence "Flo" Huntington – Jesse's sister

Captain Witherell, in charge of Fort Mackinac

       Dora Witherell Captain's daughter

       Sergeant Mauvais

       Private Abernathy, clerk

Jack Welling – Neighbor and tutored by Jesse

       Peter Welling, Jack's father

              Maude Welling, Jack's older sister

Students

       Opal Duvall – youngest of the Duvall children

       Bea Duvall

       Benjy/Bemidii – Ojibway child

Horses

       Moo is the Hadleys' brown and cream Percheron, used on Mackinac Island to pull drays

       Bear is the Hadleys' black Percheron used in summer on Mackinac Island to pull drays

       Goldy & Silver are the Huntingtons' horses purchased from the Hadleys.

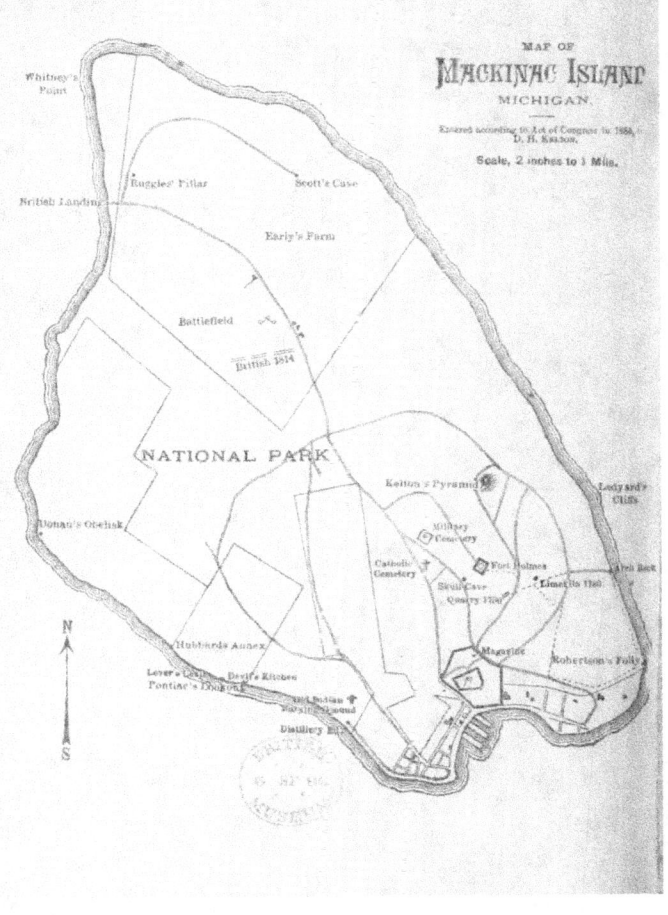

MAP OF
MACKINAC ISLAND
MICHIGAN.

Entered according to Act of Congress in 1884, by
D. H. Kenton.

Scale, 2 inches to 1 Mile.

Whitney's Point

British Landing

Ruggles' Pillar

Scott's Cave

Early's Farm

Battlefield

British 1814

NATIONAL PARK

Kelton's Pyramid

Lover's Cliffs

Nonan's Obelisk

Military Cemetery

Fort Holmes

Arch Rock

Catholic Cemetery

Skull Cave

Quarry 1760

Lime Kiln 1760

Hubbards Annex

Magazine

Robertson's Folly

Lover's Leap
Pontiac's Lookout

Devil's Kitchen

Old Indian Burying Ground

Distillery Hill

N

S

Prologue

Pickford, Michigan, Hadley Percheron Farm
May 1893

Gathering breakfast plates, Maggie Hadley peered over her father's shoulder at the *Soo Evening News'* front page headline:

COUNTRY HEADING TOWARD ECONOMIC CRISIS

Pa jabbed a stout finger at the paper. "The country might be in a crisis, but people will always need horses to pull their wagons."

Her gut clenched as her two youngest brothers exchanged a quick glance as they pushed away from the long oak table.

John brushed back a lock of auburn hair from his hazel eyes. "You haven't forgotten about those auto mobiles they are starting to build, have you, Pa?

Pa snorted. "Only a fool would think those contraptions could pull heavy drayage down the streets." He kept his gaze fixed on the newspaper, but her brothers rolled their eyes heavenward.

Maggie shot them what she hoped was a quelling look.

"We're going out to feed the horses, Pa," John called over his shoulder as they headed toward the front door.

Pa grunted.

Ma, seated to Pa's left, set her napkin on the table. "Our bank is out in that barn. All that horseflesh. No need worryin' about rich people's problems."

Pa turned and looked up at Maggie. "Your Ma is right. Go on and get those dishes started, Maggie girl, in case our company shows up early."

Ma tucked a stray blonde curl behind her ear as she rose from the table. "The Huntingtons will be here in a bit."

Pa's lips worked into a thin worry line before he turned his attention back to the paper.

Maggie strode away to the nearby kitchen and glanced out the window, into the yard. She had been warned to "Mind your P's and Q's," while the wealthy railroad owner and his son visited. And that didn't sit well with her. At twenty-one years old why should she have to be treated like a child?

Maggie set the dirty dishes on the wood counter. She pushed scraps for the dogs off into one bowl and the rest into a covered tin receptacle that they used for garbage. Then she placed the dishes into the sink. She removed the hot water from the stove and poured it over the dishes. Maggie carefully set the heavy pot back on the stove. She returned to the sink and added baking soda to the water, then swished it around with her scrub brush. Out the window she spied their two hounds chasing one another in the yard and couldn't help but grin.

Ma moved alongside her. "Those two sure love to chase each other, don't they?"

"Yes, they sure do." Beyond the dogs, her two brothers shoved each other playfully. "As do your two youngest."

Chuckling, her mother dipped her blue and white speckled coffee mug into the dishwater. "They better not engage in such behavior when that prim-and-proper college boy shows up with his father.

Scowling, Maggie began scrubbing the dishes. "Just because his father owns half of the national railroads, it doesn't give them a right to prance in here and try to buy Pa's horse stock."

Ma elbowed her gently. "I think you mean 'our' not your Pa's horse stock. This is a family business, after all." Ma, raised in Michigan's Eastern Upper Peninsula, had learned to fend for herself and perform many "men's" chores her entire life. And she obviously considered herself an equal with Pa.

"So you think Pa means it when he says all of us have a crack at running this farm? Me included?"

"Of course. And if he didn't. . ." Ma snatched a wood spoon from the dishwater and waved it around, spattering the counter with droplets. "I'd have to make my point with a rap on his noggin."

Maggie laughed. "You wouldn't."

"He won't test me." Ma tapped the spoon against her work-roughened palm.

Pa joined them. "What's that?"

"Our daughter could help run the farm one day, when you can't."

"She can try, dumpling. Doesn't mean she will." Pa winked before Ma playfully attempted to hit him with the spoon. He ducked away.

"Now wouldn't that be a good sight for Maggie's potential beau to see once he arrives?"

"What?" Both Ma and Maggie spit out the word in unison.

"Sure thing." Pa stroked his short salt and pepper beard. "Instead of selling that young college fella and his Pa any of our horses, I'll pull an old switcheroo and have him married off to Maggie in a trice."

Her mother's eyes were wide as saucers as Maggie's must be, too.

"You've plum lost your mind, Mr. Hadley." Ma shook her head and sighed.

Chuckling as he went, Pa headed toward the heavy oak front door, and closed it securely behind him.

"Well I never." Ma huffed a breath.

"As if." Maggie plunged her hands into the hot dishwater and swished the dishes around. "I suppose if they needed a maid they could consider me." *But a wife? Never.*

"Still, it wouldn't hurt for you to purty yourself up a bit."

Maggie ceased stirring the water. "Ma? Do I need to drive both you and Pa over to that new asylum in Newberry?"

"I don't think it's in operation yet." Ma smirked. "Besides which, if you drove us over there then those town folks might think you're more than a little odd yourself."

"If I were a man. . ."

"Yes, I know. If you were a man you'd be the best dray driver around. All of Pickford knows that, and they understand. But town people—"

"Another matter entirely." As Ma had said numerous times. So this was to be Maggie's' life. Washing up and doing housework instead of working outside all day long.

"I'll finish up the dishes and you go fix yourself up." Ma laughed. "At least practice some of your womanly ways on this city fella. It can't hurt."

If it got her outside and near her beloved horses then Maggie was all for it. "Yes, ma'am."

Jesse Huntington surveyed the large white wood-clad farmhouse set amidst rolling fields of verdant grass. Hardwood trees densely bordered the property. He blew an exasperated breath out. With this depressed economy, what was his father doing trying to purchase some of the Hadleys' draft horses? And since they were so busy already with railroad company business, why bother with this odd venture?

Father's anxious laughter, while conversing with the owner, frayed the edges of Jesse's own nerves.

"Mr. Hadley, do you enjoy the rustic life here?" Father's jovial tone, directed at the Percheron farm owner didn't imply condescension but still, Jesse cringed.

The bearded man, who stood a head shorter than Father, grinned—apparently taking no offense. "Love it. Love my life. Very blessed. Love all these critters." He gestured around to the massive Percherons that were getting their fill of grass in the nearby field.

"Exactly. The simple life." Father drew in a deep gulp of air. "Away from all the stench of the city."

Jesse suppressed a laugh. The air smelled strongly of horse manure emanating from the nearby open barn. But a gentle breeze did carry a tinge of fresh evergreens and hay. He'd go mad if he lived in a place like this. Now that he'd finally graduated college he'd rather be back in Father's office in the city.

Mr. Hadley shrugged. "With five sons and a daughter, it's never been a simple life."

In the distance, a drayman slapped the reins on the back of two stout draft horses and turned them onto the Hadley's property. With a straight back, a large slouch hat pulled low over his brow, and a navy bandana wrapped around his neck and mouth, the rider looked more an outlaw than a delivery man. Jesse frowned as he glanced at Mr. Hadley. Their host removed a handkerchief from his overalls' pocket and wiped his brow.

Hadley raised a suntanned hand. "Excuse me for a moment." The older man loped over to the drayman, who'd stopped about two stone's throws from the barn.

Jesse squinted, removed his eyeglasses and wiped them with his monogrammed linen handkerchief, then put them back on. A white and light blue checked shirt peeked from beneath the driver's jacket sleeves. That and his small-looking scuffed brown boots struck Jesse as odd.

Father scowled. "There's nothing on that dray. Wonder what he wants."

"Maybe he's picking up something from the Hadleys." Throughout his life, Jesse had been warned that others might try to harm them because of their prominent social position but it seemed the drayman was well-known to Hadley.

With unbelievable alacrity, the driver maneuvered the horses and dray around and back out onto the dirt road. Jesse blinked.

"Those must be some of Hadleys' horses. Strong and sure-footed. Did you see that turn they did? Exceptional." Father's mood was downright jovial today, something Jesse hadn't observed at the office.

"Yes, an exceptional turn." Was it the horses who were responsible or the driver? That took substantial skill to execute the tight turn.

Mr. Hadley rejoined them, his pleasant features tight. "Sorry about that."

Father tapped his walking stick into the mud. "Were those your horses, Hadley?"

"Yes." The man's terse tone would have dissuaded Jesse from more questions, but not Rutherford Huntington the third.

"Your driver? I've never seen anything quite like it." Father leaned in, as if expecting a reply.

Striding forward toward the barn, Mr. Hadley ignored the question and waved toward the stalls, filled with Percherons.

Two young men, attired in work clothes and floppy hats mucked out the stalls. They grinned at Jesse, and he smiled and tipped his hat back at them, suddenly feeling ridiculous in his suit. "Beautiful horses." Absolutely *unneeded* beauties though.

Here in Michigan's Upper Peninsula, the horses were too far from the Huntington's Charleston, South Carolina home. They were also an unnecessary purchase in the current difficult economy. And where he and Father needed to be was in Charleston—at work.

For the next hour, they perused the various horses. There were only four that Mr. Hadley agreed to possibly sell. Jesse ambled out of the barn and into the sunlight. He pulled his gold pocket watch, a graduation gift, from his vest and flipped the cover open. It was getting late, and they'd need to leave soon.

The farmhouse's front door opened. A slim young woman, dressed in a simple brown work skirt topped by a white apron and covered in a dark navy shawl tightly wrapped around her, trod toward them. She looked to be nearly as tall as he was, with wide shoulders. She appeared as if someone had merged what the Brits called a beautiful English rose—a woman with a pale complexion and appearing vulnerable—with that of a Viking warrior woman with strong features. The result was a juxtaposition of the best of both and caused his breath to hitch.

The beauty focused intently on Mr. Hadley, but then she cast Jesse a quick glance. He waited for a second, and the longer look that was sure to come, despite his spectacles. Most young women he met made sure they fixed him with an appreciative sustained appraisal. Some were coyer than others about it but this young woman took about as much notice of him as a fence post. A niggle of irritation worked through him. Hadn't he complained that the only thing that drew attention to him was his money, or rather his father's money? She was likely this farmer's daughter. Perhaps she didn't feel he would give her the time of day.

Since she was taking no notice of him, Jesse surreptitiously watched as she crossed her arms and paced behind her father and his own. With that aggrieved look on her face, she didn't seem any happier about this purchase than he was.

Jesse took several long strides to join the small group.

The young woman tapped Father on his shoulder. "If you live in South Carolina, like you're saying, then why would you want to buy our horses, Goldy and Silver, way up here?"

Mr. Hadley wrapped an arm around the young woman. "He'd like them for his Mackinac Island home."

"Why? You can't possibly require two Percherons to pull your carriage, sir."

Father laughed. "But I want them. They're spectacular. I love quality, my dear."

"We do have quality Percherons here, Mr. Huntington." Hadley gave his daughter what was probably supposed to be a stern look, but the young woman glared right back.

She cocked her head. "Will you stable them with us then, out of season? Goldy and Silver are accustomed to being with their pals."

Father's jowls shook as he laughed. "I like you, young lady. You'd have made a good businesswoman."

Miss Hadley jutted out her jaw. "I'm the best. . ."

Her father waved his hand, and she ceased speaking, which surprised Jesse. She seemed like the type who'd keep on talking over anyone else who got in her way. Vivienne, his younger sister could do that with such Southern charm that almost no one realized she was doing it. He suppressed a chuckle.

"Maggie, go run and have your mother bring one of the contracts from my desk in the house."

She bobbed her head once, and then ran like a man would, across the yard to the house.

So would he ever know what Maggie thought she was best at? Perhaps they'd have an invitation in for a hearty lunch—then he might learn.

Father pulled out his pocket watch and checked it. "I'll need to sign that form, pay you, and we'll need to be on our way, Mr. Hadley."

Now Jesse would never know. Unless he asked. "Excuse me Mr. Hadley, what was your daughter trying to say she was the best at?"

Both older men fixed him with a penetrating gaze that bespoke volumes. He raised his hands. "Sorry, I was curious."

"Curiosity killed the cat, Son." Father shook his head in disapproval.

"I'm not a cat."

Mr. Hadley guffawed. "You got your Pa on that one. So I'll let you in on a little secret."

Jesse leaned in. "Yes?"

"She's the county fair winner three seasons running for best jam."

"Jam?"

"Yes, sir, she is." Mr. Hadley beamed, but a tiny muscle near his left eye jumped.

Jesse had been sure she'd been about to disclose something fascinating. Something different. But somehow the disappointment he felt should have made it easier to leave. He didn't believe Miss Hadley was about to say anything about winning blue ribbons for jam making.

"Here it is!" Maggie jogged into the barn, her shawl flapping open to reveal a checked white and blue shirt. Like the breakneck speed dray driver was wearing earlier. And on her feet were similar, if not the same, brown work boots worn by the expert driver.

Jesse smiled and chuckled to himself. Miss Hadley shot him a quizzical look and he rubbed his jaw trying to stifle his delight with his discovery.

Too bad he'd never see her again.

Maggie would give any man a run for his money—or his heart.

Chapter One

Charleston, South Carolina January 1894

Jesse Huntington settled in at his home office's massive mahogany desk, which had been cleared except for one tray piled high with letters from creditors. Father's grave had barely been dug, months earlier, before they'd discovered the desperate financial straits they were in. Jesse reached for the silver personal correspondence tray, and his heart leapt when he spied Mr. Reynold's name and address on it. He slit the envelope open and pulled out the single page and scanned it. Heart sinking, he crumpled the cryptic rejection letter from Mr. Reynolds in his hand and tossed it into Father's black-leather covered wastebasket. Still no job for him. *One of my last hopes.* His jaw muscle spasmed.

The eight-paneled oak office door creaked open. Mother, attired in her expensive and frivolous black mourning gown peeked in, the wide puffed sleeves, satin fabric, and ornate lace speaking volumes about her opinion of his announcement that they must cut expenses. She clutched a newspaper in her hand as she eyed the stack of bills. "How long do you think we have?"

The sum of what was left in the accounts, and in the cash he'd kept for emergencies, would be gone in a trice if she continued spending. Not long at all, if he couldn't procure a job. "Enough time to get us up to the island and back to the. . ." He almost said, 'summer home,' but now the West Bluff cottage on Mackinac Island would be their only residence.

"To our new home. We'll still be among our own kind there—even if they're mostly Yankees." Mother sniffed. "As was your dear father."

She'd loved Father. No doubt about that. Who else would put up with his long absences and cantankerous moods? Some of Mother's devotion no doubt stemmed from having been rescued from being an impoverished Southern belle and then married to a wealthy man. Father had saved her family's estate and plantation but now both were about to be sold to pay off their creditors. "Your least favorite Northerner just sent me a one-line rejection."

"Mr. Reynolds also refused you?" Her lips compressed in anger. "Wait until I see him on the island, I'll give him a piece of my mind."

Jesse couldn't help but laugh. "Mother, your genteel calling out would likely be perceived as a compliment by him."

She likely had no idea that her soft reprimands, in her Southern belle style, would be completely lost on the Northern iron mine magnate whose vocabulary possessed an imaginative assortment of profanities. Mother blinked up at him, her right hand clutching the newspaper so tightly that it began to crumple. "The advertisement has been published."

Jesse extended his hand and accepted the paper. He opened to the appropriate section. "A Large House on the Battery." That had to be it. He scanned the notice, his chest muscles tightening as though he was taking a battery himself. He refolded the Charleston Gazette and passed it back to his mother. A house was not a home. Home would be wherever he and his family landed on their feet.

"If anyone asks you, you did take that tour of Europe your father promised you."

"I'm not going to lie." He'd worked the summer after his graduation from Harvard alongside his father. Then the horrendous hurricane had hit Charleston in late August. As Jesse and the entire family were en route to evacuate to Summerville, his father's heart failed him. "At least the house survived the hurricane relatively unscathed." *Unlike Father.*

Mother's eyes widened and she blinked back tears. "I never realized how. . ."

Jesse handed her his handkerchief and pointed to the nearby settee.

She shook her head. "I had no idea how much our so-called friends despised your father."

Jesse ducked his chin and stared down at the wool Persian rug at his feet, one of Father's favorites. "He was a Yankee." As were the Huntington children, by default. But more than that his father had turned out to be a ruthless businessman, something that Jesse hadn't realized until he'd worked directly with Father. The only time he'd seen him relaxed and generous in a business deal was when he'd bought the Percherons in Michigan. The image of a strawberry blonde young woman stamping her booted toe in the dirt came to mind.

"Well, I will always remember that first and foremost I am Camille Calhoun. Papa always told me no one could take that from me." Mother's countenance altered oddly. She laughed. "We'll enjoy our summer resort home. Then, by September, we'll be back here and the world will be set aright." She beamed up at him, a Southern belle at her most charming.

Jesse stiffened. Mother's moods had been somewhat unpredictable before Father's death, but now she was becoming irrational. Short of a miracle their world as they knew it would never be the same.

There would be no return come next autumn.

Pickford, Michigan, Hadley Percheron Farm
March 1984

Maggie sat, her heavy skirts arranged around her, on a wood bench made from two stumps topped by a wide slat of wood. She rubbed a flannel rag sopped in saddle soap into harness leather while Pa and the veterinarian from Mackinac Island looked over their Percherons. Soon it would be time to transfer the horses back to the island.

Dr. Howerter, as usual, took his time examining each draft horse. "They're all looking pretty good to me, Buck."

Pa nodded. "Wish I knew how many they're gonna contract for this year, though."

"Hard to say with the economy being what it is right now."

"It's got to turn around soon." Pa patted Bear's rump. Bear was his favorite. And he was also the horse Maggie normally used when driving the dray into town for her family's business.

"I heard your boys had to take positions elsewhere. Will they be coming back at least for the season?"

"Winter got so slow they had to take up jobs in the logging camps and over in the Soo at the new locks being built. But my two youngest will be back soon and we stipulate in our contracts that at least one Hadley will be driving dray for the Danners' dray service."

"I see. I thought you had an arrangement like that with Danner."

Maggie turned away and rolled her eyes in irritation. She was a much better driver than any of her brothers. Too bad the islanders couldn't simply look the other way, like the folks in Pickford did when she made deliveries. At five feet eight inches tall she might not compare to her over six feet tall brothers with their well-muscled arms, but she was strong enough to load and unload moderately heavy supplies.

From the open barn door, she saw their neighbor, Phillip Crist, ride in. The families took turns picking up mail when it was delivered to town. Normally Mr. Crist would be on horseback but today he was driving the mercantile owner's light carriage. As the carriage moved forward, the passenger with Mr. Crist, wrapped in a navy wool blanket, slumped forward.

It was her brother, Russell.

"Russ!" Maggie ran out of the barn and into the yard. Ma came out of the front door and the two of them moved toward the carriage, where Mr. Crist was assisting Russell down. Pa and Doc ran up and each wrapped an arm around her brother, who looked pale as death.

"What happened?"

"A tree came down on him." Mr. Crist removed his hat. "A widow-maker."

Doc gave him a sharp glance. "Then he's lucky to be alive."

"Let's get him to his room."

Hours later, they'd gotten Russell settled in his own bed where he slept comfortably. They'd also sent word to Sault Sainte Marie for a physician to ride out. Ma and Pa sipped tea and rocked in their matching ash wood rockers. "Ought to look at the mail, I reckon."

Maggie got up from the table, where she'd been peeling potatoes and brought them the twine-wrapped stack that Mr. Crist had brought from town. She returned to her task when she heard Ma gasp.

"This is from John's landlady, Mrs. Scholtus." Ma clutched the letter in her hand. "It says he's been badly injured at the Soo Locks site. Oh my poor boys!" Ma began to cry.

"Oh no!" Poor John. Poor Russ. What could she do to help them? Maggie grabbed her work coat and headed out to the barn and to her beloved horses. She had to do something.

There'd be no shared income from her brothers—what would her parents do? What could Maggie offer in the way of assistance?

She paced pass Goldy and Silver's stall but then turned back around. Mr. Huntington, their owner, had died and they'd received no payment for stabling them that winter. Pa didn't want to bother Mrs. Huntington because he'd read they'd lost their fortune. What if the Huntingtons wanted to sell Goldy and Silver to someone else who then abused them? She stepped into the stall and patted Goldy on her side and then pressed her cheek against her neck. What would the Huntingtons do? They had a contract showing the horses were theirs.

A contract.

Mr. Danner—he has a contract.

The Mackinac Island businessman would have to honor his contract this season. She could put her horse skills to good use. She could drive dray, posing as one of the Hadley boys. Because it wouldn't be only Goldy and Silver being sold by the Huntingtons—if her family couldn't take care of taxes and business expenses then the whole stable was threatened.

16

Maggie straightened and then leaned back, peering up at the barn rafters as if some other answer would come to her there. But those softly whispered words in her heart of a contract with Mr. Danner swirled around in her soul urging her to take action.

Could she?

And if she could, then what would it take?

Jesse's sister, Florence, lay with her head upon his shoulder as they rode north on what had once been one of his father's train lines. Her soft snores were no rival for the noise of the train tracks and the sounds of conversations around them. What a strange sensation to be in a regular passenger car. Mother, seated across from him, kept her eyes closed, but he knew she wasn't sleeping by the way she kept shifting in her seat. He'd covered her with a wool blanket that he'd also draped across Vivienne. His youngest sister kept busy scribbling notes on the passengers, which she'd explained was for her theatrical pursuits. He didn't bother arguing with her. Father had forbidden her aspirations and Mother was too distraught at present to discuss what Vivienne could and could not do.

He shook out his copy of the *Detroit Free Press* which included several articles about the May Day riots. He'd hoped to pursue some of Father's lesser contacts in the north for possible work, but with all this discord would it be safe to bring his family to any of those cities? He could leave the women on Mackinac Island if he procured a job in Chicago or Cleveland, and then bring them down when things calmed. But no one had yet even replied to his inquiries much less outright rejected him. He glanced at the classified section, which along with the usual search for lumberjacks and laborers also contained several teaching positions posted for hire. Now there was a lowly profession if ever there was one.

Vivienne waggled a finger at him. "A penny for your thoughts."

He exhaled sharply. "They aren't worth that much, so hang onto your money."

Her lips formed into a pout. "That's all you ever think about."

"I was talking about selling those Percheron horses not only because we could use the funds. . ." He rubbed his forehead. He must be more tired than he realized because he'd almost blurted out that he'd been discussing selling the horses so that he could go to Hadley Farms once more.

"But what?"

"Hmm?" He blinked at his sister as she twirled a long blonde ringlet around her index finger.

"If it's not about the money then what's that about?"

He gaped at her. *Because I want to see Maggie Hadley again. I want to challenge her to race her dray back into the yard again so I can tell her I know it was her.* "Because I don't like leaving things unsettled." That was true enough.

"Oh. Pooh." Vivienne blew out an exasperated breath, which puffed up the fringe of hair on her forehead. "Florence said that bill was not of much account."

He was about to correct her but thought it was better to change the topic. "I recall they have several professional theatrical companies who come to the island."

"I imagine they'll still come. People still want to be entertained to distract themselves from their difficulties."

"And they have a local theatrical group you might be able to investigate now that you'll be staying on the island year-round."

Her blue eyes widened. "When you say it like that, it sounds so real, doesn't it?"

"I'm afraid it is true. We've at least got this home, though." For how long he couldn't be sure. What would happen if he couldn't find some kind of work?

Teachers, while held in slightly higher regard, made far less wages than a lumberjack.

But such positions were considered respectable.

Was that what he'd be? Respectable?

There were far worse things.

Chapter Two

Mackinac Island, Michigan, Danner's Stables

"Mickey Hadley, sir, reporting for work." With her brother Russell's floppy workman's hat firmly atop her head, covering her hair, Maggie slunk into a hard wooden chair across from Mr. Stan Danner. The way the dray company owner glanced at her head, he no doubt thought she ought to remove her hat out of respect during this interview.

Why hadn't she thought about all the places where she'd be expected to take off her head covering? How was she to attend church services while she was on the island? She'd have to buck up and cut her hair short—maybe to her shoulders. She glanced up at the businessman from beneath her hat brim.

"Welcome, *son*." The way he drew out the word, son, sent her heartbeat skittering. Mr. Danner heaved a sigh. "Glad you could make it over. Begging your pardon, *boy*, but you appear pretty much a lightweight, which concerns me."

The stable owner was, himself, a compact but wiry man. Maggie bit back a retort and forced out her newly acquired baritone voice, "I'm a hard worker."

"So your Pa said in the letter he sent." Danner tapped an envelope on his pine desktop.

Maggie nodded.

He cocked his head at her. "With the May Day riots, I'm short of dray drivers right now, Mickey."

"Yessir, I'd heard about that." Workers were fed up with their ill treatment and had rioted to protest. "The dock workers commented upon it when I told them where I was going."

A muscle in the older man's jaw twitched. "Without your brothers we're having trouble keeping up with orders."

"My brothers told me how much they enjoyed working here."

"Hmm, yes." He rose and turned away from her, rubbing his jaw.

"The Hadleys have always tried to honor their contracts." Granted, the contract, as written was decidedly one-way with Mr. Danner being required to offer a position but the Hadleys not required to fulfill it.

The man paced by the back wall. Was he stalling? "Yes, and your Pa surely told you how that contract is written."

"Yessir." *Hadley men. Not Hadley women.* Why had Pa included that one word? One simple word that could prevent her from keeping her family from sinking. They were in desperate straits for sure. She ran her tongue over her lower lip. Surely he couldn't tell she was a young woman. And Pa said he'd never told him. Her two youngest brothers swore they'd said nothing about their sister.

"Your eldest brother, by far was one of the chattiest draymen I've ever had." Danner fixed her with his deep brown eyes.

Her heart sank down to her scuffed boots. "He loves to tell a good story. Sometimes makes up all manner of things."

The man's lips pulled together. "Like that he had a younger sister who'd make the best dray driver of all if only she weren't a woman?"

Maggie clamped her eyes shut, cringing.

Danner laughed. "Mickey is a fine name for a young lad. Has a nice ring."

His words jolted through her as she opened her eyes.

"I believe I'll give you a try." He extended his hand.

He knew. Mr. Danner knew she was Pa's youngest – a daughter and yet. . .

"You're still gonna hire me?" Maggie swallowed hard.

"That's right. You might be too young to even shave yet but I'm desperate here for drivers. I guess your Pa must be, too, eh?"

Maggie exhaled the breath she hadn't realized she'd been holding. "Yes, sir."

"I value the Hadley Percherons, and I need more drivers. I'm willing to overlook your um," he gestured to her and frowned, "youth on one condition."

Oh no. "Yes, sir?"

"Need to see your driving skills for myself. See if that eldest brother of yours is right about your skills."

She usually drove alone, but Pa and her brothers had accompanied her after she'd learned to drive. "Sure thing, Mr. Danner."

"All right, then. Let's go down to the docks and pick us up some luggage."

Luggage? Pa had said there would be a worker with Maggie to unload the bags and she'd only drive. Would Mr. Danner expect her to load and unload? Might as well find out right now if this was going to be an issue. Maggie sent up a quick prayer. "Sir, I need to let you know I'm only fit for driving and dealing with light to moderate weights, not for loading and unloading heavy goods."

"We'll tell my other customers that maybe in a few years when you've picked up another fifty pounds or so of muscle, then I'll let you deal with their cargo and baggage."

Except there wouldn't be all that muscle on her ever, which made her chuckle. "Thank you, sir."

He stood and grabbed his soft floppy cap. "We'll figure something out. In the meanwhile, I'll do the loading today and unloading and you just handle my horses." He gave her a hard stare. "Come to think of it, they're likely your own Percherons anyway."

"Yessir." Pa said that Danner's stable included dray horses that were over eighty percent from their farm.

"Come on, follow me."

Inside the huge stable, Maggie's eyes widened when she spotted Bear and Moo, from home, feeding at a trough. Bear's ears twitched and he raised his head and then he fixed Maggie with his big eyes. Moo lifted her head, too, and then flicked her tail back and forth before leaving the trough and heading toward Maggie. She stopped a foot away and then bent her head and nudged Maggie's barn coat pocket. She pulled out a carrot, palmed it, and offered it to the majestic Percheron.

"Looks like you'll get along well."

"They're my favorites." She stroked Moo's neck.

"Ah, we're not supposed to have favorites among our children or our horses." Danner winked as he, too, reached into his pocket and held out a chunk of apple for Moo. "But she's a sweetheart and there are no two ways about it."

"They both are."

"Well, let's get these two beauties ready to go."

Soon they'd hitched up Bear and Moo. Maggie and Mr. Danner mounted onto the dray. This was different than driving into town at home. Even though the island was only about six miles square, in summer there were thousands of occupants, many of whom congregated downtown not far from the stables. 'Be alert at all times,' Russell had warned her, 'this isn't a country drive.'

As she directed the horses from the stables onto the street, a stout woman clutching a blond boy's hand stepped out into traffic. Maggie brought the pair of horses to an abrupt stop. The way the woman glared at her, from beneath her wide-brimmed hat, you'd think Maggie had done something wrong, not the other way around.

"This would be regular behavior around here." Danner sighed. "But you handled that well."

They'd turned onto Cadotte Street and had traveled only a block when a pair of bicyclists, two young men wearing matching red and white striped shirts and khaki riding pants zipped in front of the dray. Maggie was ready to rein them in, but the horses acted as though nothing had happened. She'd experienced this kind of reckless behavior during summers at home, in town, too. Some people sure didn't think much about their lives.

"Turn up there and then pull over by Doud's Market."

Her brothers had emphasized where different stores and specific businesses were located to help Maggie get her bearings, otherwise she might not have seen the sign, because on the side of the business was painted an advertisement for Foley's Photography Studio. A line of carriages was parked alongside the main street as far as she could see. Bear and Moo acted happy as could be. She set the brake.

The sun broke through the cloud banks and illuminated the ship that had pulled into the harbor.

"The last of the summer crowd, I'm thinkin'." Danner scratched his cheek. "But I'm expectin' a family coming in with a full load."

"Oh." Why hadn't he said so back at the stables?

"I keep watchin' for them. but this is the last ship expected into Haldimand Harbor today, so maybe this time."

"But if they don't arrive, we'll help someone else?"

"No. If they don't arrive then we'll head up to the fort." His mouth pulled as though he was chewing on his lip. He didn't say why they'd go to the fort, but Russell had told her that a big part of his drayage job was hauling to and from the fort.

Bear's ears flicked as though he heard something that worried him. Maggie sat up straighter. Moo stomped his foot. Maggie surveyed all her surroundings. The fort's garden lay to her left. Although there weren't many soldiers still stationed there, fresh vegetables were still grown. Baby corn stalks tufted at the ground and green lacy carrot tops populated long rows.

Danner motioned to the garden's end where melon vines grew. "With our milder climate here on the island, we can grow a few more things than on the mainland."

Maggie kept her focus on her surroundings. A heavy-set man standing on the sidewalk nearby lit a cigar. Bear lifted his head and tugged but she held fast. "He doesn't like smoke." Bear had narrowly escaped a barn fire at his previous owner's home. He could ignore chimney smoke, but they kept him from open fires at home and no one smoked at Hadley Farms—it wasn't allowed.

Whistling, Danner pointed to Bear's ears. "On the island, we distract Bear by whistling or talking to him if we've got him around smokers, of which we've many."

"Good idea." Maggie watched as Bear settled right back down into his sturdy Percheron dispositional ways. He shook, jingling the metal hardware on his harness. "Do you think he's reacting more like he would at home with me here now?"

"That could be it, Mickey." Danner grasped his hat as a gust of wind threatened to carry it off.

Maggie continued to scan the street for other vehicles and pedestrians. The ship, now moored, began to disembark passengers. "I'm watching for a young dark-haired man with his mother and two sisters. All the womenfolk have reddish hair." Danner cast a look at her. "Like all you Hadley men have."

It was true. The Hadleys all had some red in their hair from strawberry blonde like hers to a flaming red like Russell's.

Maggie's hip muscles began to cramp. Truth be told, she wasn't used to waiting anywhere this long. How would she handle the position if she had to sit for hours on end? Just when she thought she couldn't stand another moment, Mr. Danner pointed to the last cluster of people leaving the boat docks. "That's the family I was speaking of. I'll hop down and run let the Huntingtons know we're here. You pull in behind that last carriage that's fixin' to leave."

"The Huntingtons?" Did that include the one man who could expose her secret? They'd lost their fortune, businesses, and home in Charleston and hadn't even paid the winter boarding fees for their horses, and yet they now arrived on the island? Perhaps it was a different family by the same name. But as she stared, gape-mouthed at the handsome dark-haired young man whose spectacles covered what she knew were beautiful hazel eyes, she swallowed hard. She needed this job.

And she wouldn't let Jesse Huntington ruin things for her.

What a different kind of journey this had been to Mackinac Island compared to years past. Jesse held tight to his boater hat as a Straits of Mackinac breeze gusted. Around him, other men did the same. Even his sisters, whose befeathered and lace-encrusted hats were secured with many hat pins, gripped their wide brims. The ship's horn startled him, and his ears rang.

Mother lifted an eyebrow at him. "I should think you'd be used to that sound after all these years."

He shrugged. His nerves were as taut as a high wire strung over a precipice. The island school hadn't sent him a reply as to when his interview would be scheduled. No interview, no job. No job, no paycheck. And very little money left. . .

"Look!" His sister Florence pointed to the dock where a queue of workers awaited to direct passengers and to carry luggage to the hotels.

This year, compared to last, there were at least twenty percent fewer porters holding wheeled luggage carts. Which wasn't bad, considering the economy. Perhaps Jesse could find something up here. Or several positions.

"First class baggage?" The heavyset porter approaching them was one Jesse didn't recognize from previous years.

"No, it's in storage below."

"Oh." The man's ruddy face altered from smiling to slight condescension, something Jesse had never experienced before their fall in society but which he experienced now all too often.

27

"At least we'll get to enjoy the season." Mother sniffed.

"How we'll do that on the allowance Jesse gave us will be a miracle." His sister Vivienne fished around in her reticule and pulled out some Dr. Fisher's Cure-All Mints, opened the tin, and offered one to each of them.

Jesse raised his hand to decline. The porter seemed to be taking his time, perhaps not expecting much of a tip. Which would be correct, given the economies Jesse had to make.

A trim man in dungarees, a navy vest, plaid shirt, and floppy cap jogged toward them.

Mother straightened. "Why it's Mr. Danner. He's the owner of the stables, you know. He's come out to greet us, y'all." She beamed as though one of her aristocratic former friends from New York had taken it upon themselves to come down to the wharf. The strange gleam in her eyes, which he'd witnessed now for months, since father's death, intensified.

Jesse didn't recognize the man. Not that he'd noticed many of the workers on the small island. When they'd come north, he'd been too preoccupied with his studies and riding rough shod over his younger sisters who were prone to getting themselves into scrapes.

As he approached, Danner slowed to a quick stride, finally stopping a few steps away from them.

"Mr. Danner!" Mother called out and extended her gloved hands as though welcoming him to her court. "How lovely to see you."

The stable owner removed his cap and dipped his chin. "Ma'am." He nodded in turn at Jesse, Florence and Vivienne.

A tiny muscle in Mother's cheek twitched as she lowered her hands to her sides. "Thank you for coming to see to our needs in person."

Danner offered a shy smile. "Happy to oblige."

In the distance, Jesse spied their baggage being removed from the ship.

Danner followed his gaze. "We'll get that picked up shortly from the porter and we'll haul it up to your. . . um, your. . ."

Mother waved her hand airily. "Our summer residence."

The stable owner frowned. "Thought you were taking up year-round residence now. Ain't that right?"

Jesse nodded slowly, locking gazes with the older man, hoping to convey that they were.

Grabbing Jesse's arm, Mother glanced between Mr. Danner and himself. "We're expecting my son to set things aright soon. He'll probably be taking us to New York in the fall once he's landed a proper position there."

Mother had always embellished the truth. She claimed such exaggeration was her birthright as a Southern belle. But lately, she seemed to actually believe her lies. He'd have a chat with her later. He patted her hand. "For now, we are indeed taking up life on the island, Mr. Danner. And thank you for your assistance in getting us settled."

If Jesse didn't find a position soon they would indeed be leaving the island or at least he would – to go wherever he could procure employment. A pang of regret cinched his chest. Father was gone and many of his cronies had also lost their fortunes. The ones who hadn't gone bust were circling the wagons and hiring their own family members. Many had indicated that Father's brutality in business dealings was now being returned to his son. Sins of the father and all that.

Soon the porter rejoined them, and Jesse tipped him a modest but fair amount. Mr. Danner took their belongings and pointed toward his dray, parked across the street near the market. The driver seated atop the dray tugged a scarf up around his face despite the warm day and shifted in his seat. Strange behavior, but Jesse needed to focus on getting his family settled.

Mother leaned in. "Dear, it's over a mile to the cottage."

Jesse fingered the coins in his pocket that had been saved in case they required a taxi. Although he'd warned Mother and his sisters repeatedly that they'd have to walk up to their home to save money, he couldn't bring himself to make them travel the distance on foot. A year ago, one of their servants would have directed their driver to bring their private carriage down to retrieve them. Now, though, their driver hadn't been rehired and their carriage sat gathering dust in the carriage house. The stables were empty. That thought triggered the recollection that he'd not paid the Percheron's boarding fee. Somehow, some way, he would travel to the Hadleys' Farm and take care of the matter. How, he didn't know. Why he felt compelled to do so he wasn't quite sure. If he was honest with himself, he knew the answer, but. . .

Florence nudged him from behind with her reticule. "What are you waiting for?"

Jesse removed his arm from Vivienne's, shoved his glasses up his nose and waved at a taxi driver.

Vivienne's eyes widened. "Do you mean we can take the taxi?"

"Of course." Florence moved alongside them and tugged at her short cape.

Vivienne slipped her arm back through his. "I knew you'd come around."

Mother patted his arm. "Dear, we can't be treated like peasants. It simply won't do." Her patronizing smile skewered his heart. She still couldn't accept how dire their straits were.

The driver, a tousle-haired man in his early forties, named his fee and Jesse swallowed. It was a pittance compared to his old allowance, but expensive considering his now-limited means. He handed over the coins and then assisted the women up into the coach.

As they traveled on the back streets and then up the incline to the lane past the Grand Hotel and on toward the West Bluff cottages, Jesse's spirits sank. He'd expected to be relieved to be here. But with no job, and their assets quickly dwindling, their remaining home might soon have to be sold. Heat prickled his forehead, and he wiped his brow.

"Are you well, dear?" Mother patted his hand. "It's rather chilly out for you to look so feverish."

Florence cast him a quick glance. "He's likely sweating out how he'll feed all of us, Mother."

"Florence!" Vivienne's pixy face contorted into shock. "Don't even tease about such things."

Jesse met his youngest sister's pleading gaze. "Florence is what you might call a humbug."

"Ha!" Florence glared at him. "Humbug, I say."

Vivienne giggled. "She is, isn't she?"

"I didn't raise you girls to behave in such a manner." Mother lifted one genteel eyebrow and both sisters laughed.

"Father did." Florence tugged at the fingers of her gloves, as though straightening them, a nervous habit of hers. "He always told me to face facts squarely and unafraid."

But when her cheeks reddened, and Florence turned to look out the window, Jesse spied a tear trailing down her face. He closed his eyes. *God, if you're out there, I could use some help.*

The carriage abruptly stopped. Jesse reached across his mother to prevent her from propelling forward and across the aisle toward his sisters, both of whom clutched the edge of their seat with one hand and their hats with the other.

"Jack Welling, I near to killed you!" The driver called out as a slim boy drove by on a too-large blue bicycle. With a pinched pale face and sad eyes, Jack reminded Jesse of his own reflection in the mirror that morning. The Wellings, or rather the Swaines who were the boy's grandparents, owned a beautiful yellow home on the cliff, not far from their own. Young Jack's parents owned and operated the Winds of Mackinac, in town.

The carriage once again moved on and soon they'd arrived at their cottage. Heady lilac scent greeted them from the blooming lilac bushes and trees that dotted the entire property. Soon their spectacular roses would blossom as would the hydrangeas that banked around their wide front porch. The two-story Queen Anne style home sat back from the street with maple trees affording it some privacy from passersby.

Jesse climbed out of the carriage and then helped his family down. Although he could ill-afford to tip the driver, the man had well-earned it by stopping quickly and sparing the lad in the street. What if he'd hit young Welling? Could Mother hold up under any further trauma? She stood now, as she always did upon their arrival, hands clasped at her waist, inspecting the gardens and exclaiming upon the loveliness she found there. Vivienne cavorted around like a spring lamb while Florence crossed her arms over her chest and tapped her booted foot as she stood by the door, waiting for it to be unlocked. Jesse slipped coins into the driver's hand and then heaved a sigh.

Almost as soon as the carriage departed, the dray arrived. Mr. Danner sat alongside the driver, smiling. The driver's eyes appeared stricken. What could possibly be so terrifying? When the youth looked up directly at Jesse and his scarf slipped down his face, instant recognition jolted through Jesse. That was no boy. He took two steps back, and almost tripped over one of the planters beside the walkway. He continued to watch the dray driver. What was Miss Hadley doing driving a dray on the island? She pulled her neck scarf up again and Jesse retreated.

Jesse fumbled in his pocket for the house key, finally retrieving it and then dropping it onto the damp ground.

Florence whirled around on the porch. "Aren't you going to unlock this door?"

Mother's shocked expression and her retrieval of another house key from her reticule must have quelled Florence's ire because she now wore a contrite expression. "Florence, I am yet the head of the household, not your brother. I shan't have you shrieking at either of us like a fishmonger. . ."

Jesse didn't catch the end of the sentence. Purposefully, he turned and followed the dray around to the back, where they'd unload. Maybe he'd made a mistake. Maybe she had a brother who'd possessed a face too pretty for a man. Jesse had seen such things before.

He watched as the dray driver climbed down from the dray rather than jumping down as most men would do. An image came to mind of Vivienne, at Day School in Charleston, engaged in one of her many theatrical productions. Vivienne playing the part of a boy. These were difficult times. Desperate times for many. The May

Day riots had shown that. If Vivienne and Florence were on their own and couldn't get work as a woman what might they resort to? He didn't want to allow his mind to go there.

What would Miss Hadley need to pass as a young man? She'd need some dirt or theatrical makeup to hide the lack of any facial hair and to conceal the feminine contours of her high cheek bones. And while she wore two layers of shirts, they'd be too heavy if the sun burst from behind the clouds again. But she'd need one shirt to cover and another atop that to disguise. Something lighter for warmer days that were sure to come. Jesse rubbed a hand over his aching brow. He had enough females to concern himself with, why was he seeking out trouble? Better to accept that Miss Hadley wished to portray herself as a "lad" and go along with "his" act and maybe to even applaud it. But assist? He could barely manage his own family. Still, his natural inclination was to help. If he could. And right now he could assist with the baggage. He rolled up his shirt sleeves.

"If you and I unload, Mr. Danner, then I should be able to bring these belongings into the house on my own." Jesse jerked a thumb toward the back of the dray.

"Sure thing, young man." Danner grinned. "My new driver only handles the smaller bags. He's young and has some filling-out to do but he's a fine driver."

Jesse blinked rapidly, as he resisted the urge to raise his eyebrows in disbelief. Meanwhile, the driver turned 'his' back to them, fists on slim hips apparently surveying the load. Inhaling deeply, Jesse joined in, pulling the heavier baggage forward.

Soon the three of them had the luggage unloaded. Mother brought a wardrobe trunk, a coat trunk, and several others with heaven only knew what inside. Jesse packed five crates of his books, his basic clothing needs, and a typewriter. Vivienne surprisingly had conveyed only one trunk of clothing and another trunk of costumes, fabrics, and her sewing machine. Florence took along one small box of clothes and hats plus a large portfolio of father's business papers which the family hadn't yet finished reading. Then there were sundry boxes that held who knew what, most of which the driver carried to the back entryway.

When the dray driver remounted up onto the seat, Jesse resisted the urge to assist her. What he should have been doing was carrying some items into the back of the house. Instead, he gaped up at Miss Hadley and she turned and caught him staring. Her mouth parted, revealing even pearly white teeth. Her face, striking despite her cloud of hair hidden beneath a hat and a scarf pulled up to her chin. He looked hard at her, trying to imagine if someone who'd not previously met her would immediately know she was a female. He fisted and then unfisted his hands at the injustice of a young woman having to put herself into what could be a dangerous situation. He'd have to look out for her. *Somehow. Some way.* Her face reddened and she averted her gaze.

"What's your name, lad?"

She ducked her chin and mumbled, "Hadley. Mickey Hadley."

"Nice to meet you, Mickey."

She didn't look up.

Mr. Danner waved. "He's the youngest brother of the usual fellas who drive for me. And he drives just as good as them, too! First day on the job and I'd say Mickey is a keeper."

"Congratulations, Mickey. Thanks for bringing our belongings up for us."

She nodded then whistled and moved the huge Percherons around in a tight circle and directed them back down the drive alongside the house.

As they went, Jesse couldn't help the concern growing in his heart. He'd make sure he paid off the horses' board to her family as soon as he could.

Somehow.

Lord provide. I know you can.

Chapter Three

Maggie stewed in her own juices as she drove the dray back. The very handsome Jesse Huntington wasn't supposed to be anywhere near Mackinac Island this summer. What was he doing here? And he recognized that Maggie was a Hadley daughter passing herself as a son. And if he knew then who else would figure it out? Not something she wanted to contemplate.

Beside her in the dray, Mr. Danner nodded in approval as she had the pair of horses navigate a tricky turn. "Good job. Like a seasoned driver."

Her cheeks heated at the unexpected compliment. "Thank you."

"One of the biggest challenges to the dray drivers is managing these wide turns while watching for tourists walking, bikes darting in and out, and other carriage riders.

Not to mention those riding their horses as though they were on an outing in the woods when they were in fact in downtown traffic. Her brothers had shared their experiences with her, but it was her own trips to Pickford, which could be a busy small town on market day, that had honed her skills. "It can be tricky, but I do love driving." Maggie couldn't help but grin as she directed Bear and Moo to make the wide left turn into the stable.

"Fine job today, Mickey." Mr. Danner patted her shoulder.

When they came to a stop, she prepared herself for the rest of the work that would come. Mr. Danner hopped down.

Maggie touched the brim of her hat. "Sir, since this is my team would you need me to go ahead and take care of Bear and Moo?" That would normally be expected.

He rubbed his chin. "Seems to me that this being your first day we'll have Leonard and Jerry help you out." He waved two tall dark-haired young men forward.

She exited the dray and moved forward to rub Moo's side. Later, she'd spend some time with them in their stalls. They had a special connection, and she was awfully glad to be with them again.

The first of the men extended his hand to her. "I'm Len Zandi and that's my little brother Jerry."

Maggie hoped her handshake was firm enough, but the man's large hand dwarfed hers. If he noticed, nothing showed on his even features.

Jerry Zandi wiped his hands on his red handkerchief and didn't offer a handshake. "Heard you were from Pickford. We're from down the road a piece in Newberry."

"Nice to meet you." She kept her voice low, like she'd been practicing.

The two men set about unharnessing the team.

"First timers." Danner leaned in. "But they've been taking good care of Moo and Bear, and I'd prefer to allow them to continue to do so."

"Yes, sir."

Something in the man's dark eyes told her these brothers needed the work. "If you're as good a driver as I sense you are, you might be able to help me train them to drive the dray. I can't spare the time myself right now nor can any of the other drivers."

Maggie dipped her chin in acknowledgement. "And if you need someone to clean tack, any extra work, I can do that, too." She hoped she didn't sound too eager.

"Sure thing." Danner scratched his cheek. "Follow me and I'll show you where you can bunk down until the cold weather sets in."

Maggie had heard from her brothers that bathing could be a problem for her but that since Mr. Danner had always given the Hadleys a private space, she might be able to manage. She followed her employer to a small rectangular room at the far right of the barn behind the office area. He opened the door and waved her pass. The room wasn't much better than a stall, with a narrow bed on one wall.

"We'll move you up to one of the servants' rooms at Winds of Mackinac once the season ends. Tends to get a might chilly at night in August." A shadow passed over his face. "We've had a spell of illnesses this past year."

He opened the trunk at the base of the bed and pulled out a pillow and three blankets. "This should keep you plenty warm, but you let me know if not."

She nodded. The room was already cool and damp even in daytime.

"When it's time for a bath you go over to the back of Winds of Mackinac and let them know and they'll fix you one up that night when their laundry time is over."

"Yes, sir."

"You'll take your meals at Rosie's."

That café was a good twenty minutes by foot. If she spent forty minutes to and from that didn't leave much extra time. She had a routine of prayer and Bible study at night. It would be awfully nice to explore the island, too.

"They'll give you a box lunch to take with you and a good discount on your dinners if you take them there."

"I plan to pick up something at the market for supper. Might I be able to eat in my. . ." She almost said 'stall', "my room?"

"Sure thing. But you might enjoy eating out by the water a might better. That's where your brothers liked to eat. Down at Fairy Beach is a popular spot."

"Thank you. They made up a little map for me." Mackinac was often referred to as Fairy Island and she couldn't wait to lunch at Fairy Beach.

"We'll get you an official stable map, too." Danner inclined his head toward the exterior wall. "We're right next door if you need anything at all. Night or day."

Although he surely meant to reassure her, Danner's fatherly tone of concern had the opposite effect.

Jesse rose from his desk and stretched. He'd given his typewriter a good workout with more employment queries to companies in the Midwest. Two nights with a cool breeze ruffling the curtains had done him a world of good. He'd not realized how much the Southern climate had sapped his energy when heat and humidity encompassed Charleston. Always, in the past, he'd looked forward to the relaxing season on the island. Now, though, he needed that extra stamina to track down employment.

A light rap on the door sounded, recalling days when one of their former servants would be announcing breakfast. Instead, Florence stood there, an apron covering her drab skirt, her shirt sleeves rolled up. "Egg, cheese, and ham casserole."

"Any toast?"

40

Florence snorted and turned on her heel before heading back into the hall. Yesterday's attempt at toasted bread resulted in black briquettes being tossed out into the garbage and the house filled with the scent of Florence's failure. Mother had demanded that they send to Mrs. Christy's Tea Shoppe and Bakery for baked goods, but Jesse had quashed that habit before it got a chance to form.

At least they had a loaf of bread left from Doud's Grocery. Jesse had never considered how much he personally consumed until Florence's hand had slapped his away from the bread plate at dinner the previous night. "You have a two piece per day allowance," she'd warned him.

Maybe he should get Florence to dress up like one of the soldiers at the fort. It wouldn't take much for her to fit in up there and they'd no doubt feed her. He laughed as he imagined his take-charge sister having to submit to her superior officers' orders. That wouldn't last long until she'd be court-martialed out for insubordination.

As he headed down the hall, someone knocked at their front door. He cringed. There was no butler, nor would there be one. Not now. Maybe not ever again. That was a hard reality to accept. He opened the door, trying to remove the scowl from his face.

Jack Welling stood on the porch, hat in hand and wringing it as though it was full of water. He rocked side-to-side.

"May I help you, Jack?"

The boy peered past him, into the house. "Where's all your help?"

Jesse exhaled loudly and crinkled his nose. "I've locked the servants all in the carriage house. They're quite annoying this year for some reason. I've already had about enough of their whining."

The boy's eyes widened. "That ain't nice."

"No, it isn't nice, but it is what was needed." He winked at him. "Do you hear them yelling back there?"

Jack stood stock still for a moment. Then he bolted from the porch and around the back of the house. Jesse stepped onto the porch, ruing that his eggs would soon be cold. Possibly inedible. In the distance, a ship steamed toward the harbor. How many of their fellow West Bluff residents would arrive today?

The boy sped back around the corner, panting.

"Jack, how long have you known me?" Jesse made a comical face, his fists planted on his hips. "Would I ever make up a silly story?"

The boy scowled but then laughed. "That's a good one. But what did you really do with them?"

Jesse coughed, covering his mouth with his fist.

"I betcha got 'em down in one of the caves, right?"

He and Jack had made up some incredible stories over the years when the boy had visited them, often showing up unannounced at the Huntington's home requesting, "Story time with Jesse."

"That's right. Our entire staff is chained on the back side of the island." He shrugged. "Almost ran out of good strong chain but I stole some from a neighbor. I couldn't keep staff who were so. . ."

"What did they do?"

Jesse leaned in and whispered, "They woke me too early on my first day back."

The boy made a face of disbelief. "That ain't good enough."

"Well, indeed it isn't enough trouble to chain them up, but I was in a terrible mood." And that part of his story might be true. He was fast becoming a curmudgeon.

"No, no." Jack swiped at the air. "That ain't enough of a good reason for your story."

"Ah. It's the story you complain about."

The door opened and they both turned to see Florence. She glared at them. "Either come in here and eat or have it out here before the eggs turn stone cold."

Jack took a step forward. "Not yet Flo. I need to know a good reason why your servants ain't here. And why they've been chained in a cave on the back of the island."

Florence's mouth dropped open. Then she squared her shoulders. "Every single one of them had bet in town at the tavern that you, Jack Welling, wouldn't win the race next weekend."

"Are you serious? I'm gonna win!" He slapped his hat against his thigh.

"Well of course you will." Jesse patted the boy's shoulder.

Florence crossed her arms. "My sister and I and Jesse corralled all of those foul people, and we had Mr. Danner's new driver take them all to the cave."

"Until they come to their senses." Jesse winked at the boy, whose serious expression suggested he almost believed the story. "We had to avenge their slur on your abilities."

"Oh. Well, that makes sense." Jack turned as if to go. "Wait, I gotta ask something."

Jesse closed his eyes for a moment. Jack could turn story telling into an all-day venture if he was allowed. "What's that?"

"My dad wants you to tutor me." Jack wriggled his nose in disdain.

Digesting that request, grateful that Mr. Welling obviously hadn't shared the Huntington's plight with his son, Jesse nodded.

"So you will?"

"Yes, he will." Florence tugged at Jesse's arm, pulling him toward the door. "Come back later Jack and give us the specifics."

As soon as Jesse was inside, he fixed his sister with a long gaze, but she simply rolled her eyes at him and stalked off toward the dining room. Mother would have fainted had she observed Florence's demeanor on the porch.

When Jesse joined his sisters and mother at the long rosewood dining table, Florence glared at him before pointing to his plate, which she'd put at Father's spot. Jesse slid the plate and silverware over to his own seat. He wasn't his father. And he'd have to find his own way.

But how did he do that when every path seemed blocked?

Chapter Four

Maggie opened her bleary eyes to soft sunrise light filtering through the square window over her narrow bed. Elsewhere, tourists and summer residents were no doubt still sleeping in their comfortable lodgings. She threw off the itchy gray wool blanket and lowered her feet to the hay-strewn wood floor. Maggie drew in a breath and immediately began sneezing. How nice it would be to have indoor plumbing, like Pa had installed at home this past year. She'd thought her days of outhouses were over. But that was not to be. First she'd wash up before she headed to the necessary.

Every morning for the past three days, Maggie's face had literally been a sight for sore eyes. She stood and took two steps toward the small wall mirror. Today was no exception – red, swollen eyes reflected back at her. Beneath the mirror sat a square walnut table upon which her pitcher and bowl stood. She poured water into the basin, dipped her washcloth into it, then she patted her eyes. She'd never had swollen eyes like this happen at home. It must be from sleeping in a barn.

"Oh no," she groaned. This would not do. *Not at all.*

Between the noises from the nearby hotel boarding house, the horses in their stalls, and from sneezing much of the night, Maggie hadn't gotten much sleep her first few days. When she did slumber, Jesse Huntington kept showing up trying to help her—and he treated her like a lady, which she really couldn't have happening. So that resulted in nightmares she sure didn't need.

She dressed quickly, pulled her brother's jacket from a hook and headed off.

When she returned to the stables, she found Mr. Danner speaking with a tall strapping young man who was stroking Bear's neck. As she approached them, the stranger smiled at her, his light eyes sparkling with good humor. He stepped away from Bear and extended his broad hand as she reached them. "Eli Mitchell, nice to meet you Mickey."

Mickey gave his hand a firm shake back. "Good to meet you, too, Eli."

"Eli will be your partner on the days you're not delivering to the fort." Mr. Danner patted Eli's shoulder. "You're ready for solo outings but I'm keeping you on the easy routes for now, as we discussed."

"Yes, sir." Today she'd deliver her first dray load to the large limestone walled fort atop the hillside.

"Since you're new, that's a fairly direct route. And you'll encounter no trouble with those soldiers unloading the goods. They unload them mighty quick. It's part of the contract with me that those soldiers do all the lifting, so you stay right in your seat and let them do their work."

Eli nodded. "They'll pull off everything lickety-split." He brushed his hands quickly together to illustrate.

That was what she needed. But how was she going to manage on the days Eli rode with her? Would he guess her secret?

Danner winked at her. "Best get on your way, Mickey."

Now hours later, Maggie pulled the team to a halt outside the fort's gates, high on the hill at the back entrance. A scrawny blond-haired soldier who couldn't be much more than eighteen, held up his hand.

"Stadte yur bizihnez!" Blue eyes flashed in his narrow ruddy face. From his accent, she'd guess he hailed from an eastern European nation. Mr. Danner said over a third of the men were born outside the United States.

Spitting to the left of the dray, Maggie hoped she gave the impression of an irritated male dray owner. "What's it look like, soldier?"

The private stomped forward. "Vant you I report for dizreespeck?"

"No, sir, I wanta get this stuff in here and out so I can come back up with another load."

Apparently she'd spoken too fast because the young man blinked up at her, his cheeks reddening further.

She leaned forward and spoke in a slow, deep voice. "I got more loads to bring back."

"Goot." He rubbed his face, which looked almost as smooth as her own. "Know yur way?"

"All the way back around to the left." The Quartermaster's building was located there.

"Goot. You go." He waved her through.

Maggie exhaled a long slow breath as she clucked her tongue at Moo and Bear. Soon they were inside the gates. She glimpsed a handful of uniformed soldiers carrying rifles. They marched in formation on the green lawn at the center of the square of buildings inside the fort. A chestnut-haired young woman watched the men. Attired in a filmy white dress, tied with a pink bow at the waist, the beauty stood at the edge of the field and clutched her wide-brimmed pink hat to her head. As the dray moved closer, its wheels crunched over crushed white limestone rock. The young lady turned and faced Maggie. She waved languidly and smiled. The soldier directing the others, with stripes on his sleeve frowned. He stroked his handlebar moustache and shot Maggie a glare. She flinched. The young woman turned back around and appeared to be giggling. The mustachioed man's cheeks reddened.

Ahead of her, a soldier carrying a wooden tray filled with papers glanced between her and where the men were marching. When the soldier reached the dray he laughed. "Best not even think of breathing the same air that the captain's daughter does."

Maggie puffed out a breath. "I sure won't."

"You're new here, right?"

Maggie nodded.

"I'm the captain's clerk, Private Abernathy. I can tell you right now Dora Witherell is a whole lot of trouble."

Keeping her chin ducked low, Maggie prayed she was believable as a young man. "She looks a might long in the tooth for me, sir."

"Only twenty." Abernathy pointed back toward the gate. "Didn't stop her from flirting with Private Belsky, and he's only sixteen."

"Sixteen?"

"He lied about his age to get in. His folks need the money. And I tell you what, with all the men out in the streets trying to find work I think you and I can count ourselves lucky, can't we?" Abernathy raised his eyebrows high.

Maggie dipped her chin.

Movement in the distance caught her eye. The brunette strode purposefully toward them. *Oh no.*

The soldier's eyes widened. "You best get on to where you're going unless you want a shiner from Sergeant Mauvais."

"No, sir. I mean, yes, I best move on. Thank you, Private Abernathy."

"You can call me Abernathy, everyone does." With a gap-toothed grin, he turned and called out to the approaching woman as Maggie directed the team on, her heart beating rapidly.

Great, exactly what Maggie didn't want to happen—she'd been noticed. She was supposed to be well in the background. And now not only had she been spotted by a flirtatious female, a perturbation if there was one, but the mean-looking sergeant apparently thought Dora was his domain.

What had happened to 'Steer clear of situations and keep your head down,' which had been the advice Pa and Mr. Danner had given her? First Jesse Huntington shows up and now this young 'lady,' what next? Her hair, tightly wound around her head and hidden under her large hat began to irritate her. That long hair had to go. What if her hat blew off? She couldn't chance yet another problem. She'd already procured a pair of sheers from the town mercantile. She chewed her lower lip. Why was she worried about what Jesse might think?

Maggie directed Moo and Bear to move forward. She kept her attention focused on the trail that led behind the main buildings and away from the parade grounds. But somehow she felt Sergeant Mauvais' gaze burning through her until she rounded the corner, and he could no longer see her. She exhaled a long breath.

What happened to Mr. Danner's assertion that this would be an easy assignment?

The soda shoppe, on the main street, a favorite of Jesse's, hadn't seemed so far from the bluff when he was brought by his family's private carriage. But today he'd had to walk past the Grand Hotel, keeping his hat low on his brow, not that the wealthy therein would stoop to recognize one of their fallen. Then he'd traversed down the hill and to the sidewalk on the road that circled the island, which eventually became Main Street in town. At this pace, his shoe leather would wear out before summer was over.

He neared the Winds of Mackinac and looked around the front yard for signs of Jack, who was supposed to meet him soon. No sign of the boy nor his pretty sister, Maude, but their gardener, bent over a rosebush, shot him a scowl. "If ya ain't stayin' here keep movin' on by."

Had Jesse stooped so low in station that even a laborer thought he could chastise him? He'd have a word with Mr. Welling about the gardener when he got a chance.

Continuing on, he wove between tourists on the sidewalk. He passed an "Indian Relics" shop and May's Fudge Shop, and his bearings began to shift and settle into place. Same old Mackinac Island that he knew and enjoyed. He spied Al's Soda Shoppe ahead, a great place to treat his sisters and experience some of the local charm, since many islanders frequented the place. When the family had other social activities solely for his sisters, Jesse had been free to visit Al's place on his own. He'd enjoyed sitting in the back corner, where he could read his books and enjoy a phosphate or two. Today, though, he'd donned dress slacks, a shirt and tie, and a vest. He left his jacket behind. He didn't want to seem too formal for his tutoring session with Jack.

When he opened the door, the bells jingled. Inside only two customers, a pretty blonde woman and one of the officers from the nearby fort, sat at a small table the furthest from the door. Soon there would be no soldiers in active duty on the island, once the fort closed.

The owner looked up from folding dark green napkins into a neat pile. "Mr. Huntington, welcome back."

"Thank you, sir."

The shop owner arched a silver eyebrow at him. "I hear you're tutoring my great-nephew."

"I am."

The man chuckled. "Good luck with that one. He'd rather run or ride his bike than sit in a chair."

"What about a booth? Would he stay put there?" Jesse gestured toward a booth adjacent the wall and took his seat.

"I'm not a bettin' kind of man, but odds aren't good that he'll show up here no matter what he told you."

Jesse exhaled a quick breath. Jack Welling had always seemed to like him a great deal. At least the child enjoyed Jesse's stories. "I'll have a soda water please." He plunked down the cost indicated on the small chalkboard sign.

"Have a seat, I'll bring it to you. As you can see we're mighty slow today."

Was the economy having that kind of impact or was it because the season wasn't fully in swing? The town had seemed scantly occupied with vacationers this morning, but their family didn't usually arrive so early in the season. Jesse slid into the booth.

Al brought him his drink as Jesse was glancing at his pocket watch. "What'd I tell you, Mr. Huntington? Jack will leave you high and dry and then laugh when he finds out you waited for him."

Jesse arched an eyebrow at the older man.

When the bell jingled again, Jesse couldn't help but grin. Al stared, gape-mouthed, as Jack ran into the shop, the door slamming behind him.

"I ain't late am I?" The boy slid into his seat, across from Jesse.

Jesse shrugged. "No, you're right on time."

"Whew, good." Jack beamed. "Maude's boyfriend, Grayson, bet my dad that I wouldn't make it."

Al shook his head as he walked to the counter, lifted a hinged section, and stepped back behind.

"Really? He made a wager?" Jesse waggled his eyebrows at the boy, who laughed.

"Only because I wouldn't let him—that old Grayson—tutor me."

"Why not?"

Jack's nose twitched. "He's boring."

Jesse leaned back against the booth's wooden back, his shoulders connecting with the cool wood. "I can't guarantee I won't be the same."

"Ha. It ain't your nature as my teacher says." Jack's gamine face tugged into a scowl. "But what does he know? He says it isn't in my nature to learn to write a decent paper."

"He said that?" Jesse scowled, wanting to adjust that teacher's attitude.

"My dad helped get rid of him after Maude told him about it."

"That's good you have a sister who speaks up for you."

"Yeah, when she's not busy helping everyone else." Jack sniffed.

"Well, young sir, I, your humble servant, Jesse Huntington, am here for you now." Jesse sipped his drink.

Al returned and slid a napkin onto the table and then placed a cherry phosphate atop it. Then he reached into his heavy green apron pocket and pulled out another napkin and made a display of unfolding it and laying it atop Jack's lap. "In case of spillage."

"Thank you Uncle Al." But as soon as the man turned his back, Jack pulled a face. He leaned in and whispered,

"He thinks I'm a clumsy oaf ever since I tipped over a full glass of cider during the Autumn Festival."

"How long ago was that?" Jesse sipped his soda water.

Jack swiped his sleeve back and forth across his nose, as if scratching it. "A long time ago."

"How long?"

"Last fall." Jack dropped his arm and crinkled his nose. "And I wouldn't have knocked it over if Bea Duvall hadn't tried to grab the last donut right when I had already reached for it."

A conversation about, 'Ladies first,' would have to ensue another day. Today they were going to review their summer plan. "Is this Autumn Festival a regular event?"

"Yup." Jack leaned over his phosphate and downed a prodigious amount of the fizzy red beverage.

If he remained on the island, Jesse would find out a lot more about what went on year-round. "All right then. I better get started, because I have a lot I wanted to ask you today."

An hour later, after much review, Jesse had a much better idea of where they'd need to focus their scholarly attentions.

Jack stood and stretched. "Whatcha doin' this afternoon?"

Hopefully today the school superintendent might finally send a note to him, for an interview. Jesse slid from the booth as the front door to the shop opened and a group of five men entered, all in dark suits. He recognized Mr. Welling and smiled and nodded at him.

Jack ran toward his father and threw himself into his arms. Welling patted his son on his tawny head.

"Jesse and I have big plans and I'm gonna be readin' and writin' well before school starts back."

Jesse coughed into his fist.

"Is that so?" One of the men, who appeared to be in his fifties, with a wide girth, moved away from the group and toward him. "Might you be Jesse Huntington then?"

Jesse extended his hand to the man, whose firm grip belied his apparent soft life. "Yes, sir."

"I've been meaning to contact you. I'm Beckett Nouri, the Superintendent of Schools." His dark gaze pierced Jesse's. "I'm glad you really made it to the island."

How should Jesse reply to that strange comment? "Yes, sir." He was there. Obviously Nouri didn't think he'd show up.

"Well good, then. Come by the office later this afternoon and we'll chat."

Did that mean an interview? "Yes, sir. Thank you."

"Glad to run into you." Nouri turned to rejoin the others, who'd edged up to the counter and placed orders.

Island life. Was that how things would work then? Something inside him reminded of the peace he'd felt when he'd approached the shop earlier. Something bigger than himself was at work.

Something he'd not given a lot of thought to before now.

Chapter Five

After a week sleeping in the stable's "bedroom" Maggie's eyes were swollen nearly shut. And breathing was difficult until she was halfway through the day and outside away from the barn. Today would be her third outing with Eli Mitchell, for a dray job up on the East Bluff. She strode up to her team and patted Moo's head. He gave her a nudge and she laughed. "Moo, I don't know what I'd do without you." Every night she visited the two horses and shared all her woes. They were good listeners.

She climbed up into her seat.

"I'm here." Eli called out as he jogged toward them.

He jounced up onto the bench seat of the dray, beside her. "You look like you fought with a Michigan bobcat."

Maggie grunted. "And the bobcat won."

The young man laughed. His banter during their drives had made it easier to endure the long days. "If Abigail ever saw me lookin' like that I think she might run."

"Ha. Your wife would know you anywhere." The newlyweds were so preoccupied with one another that Maggie was grateful. Eli's thoughts were mostly on his wife, and he loved to speak about the dark-haired beauty who'd captured his heart.

"That might be." He rubbed his square jaw. "But seriously, Mickey, you better see Doc Cadotte about your eyes."

Maggie urged Moo and Bear to moved forward out of the barn and onto the street. "Can't afford a doctor."

The wagon wheels creaked as they rolled out into an opening in traffic. "Maybe you better find someplace else to lay your head at night."

Free was free. She had to keep this job. "I need to find something to fix my symptoms."

Eli slapped his hand against his forehead. "The Huntingtons."

Maggie's hands jerked against the lines and the horses slowed. Then she forced her hands to a relaxed hold. "What about them?"

"My Abigail is friends with the youngest girl. They're gonna be in a stage production together next month." Eli gushed as though this was the first time she'd heard about this event.

In fact, Maggie had heard about Abigail's role repeatedly since the first time Eli had ridden with her. "Thank you again for that ticket to the play but what does that have to do with me?"

"Vivienne, that's Miss Huntington's given name and she told Abigail to call her that, she said she desperately needs a driver." Eli guffawed. "I love how Abigail says that word, desperately."

Maggie resisted the urge to roll her eyes. "The Huntingtons don't have horses, do they?" As well she knew.

"Vivienne says her older sister is working out a way to get them back on the island, if they can find a driver."

Which meant the Huntingtons would have to pay off the winter fees. Ma and Pa would be able to put some aside for taxes. Then Maggie's wages could go toward the feed for the horses for the coming winter. "I still don't see what that has to do with me." She'd not told her dray mate, Eli, how desperate things had gotten for the Hadley family.

"Here's the thing—Vivienne wants to find a part-time driver who will receive room and board."

"Is the room in a barn?" Maggie turned her head to the side and sneezed.

"In a carriage house, so not quite as bad. And it's upstairs and enclosed. One of them fancy two-story deals like Abigail and I live in."

"I'll talk to Mr. Danner about it." Would he allow her?

"Your free time is your own. You tell Miss. . . Vivienne what hours you're available. Negotiate the deal."

"Thanks, Eli."

Eli jabbed a sturdy elbow in Maggie's side, and she tried not to wince. "We fellas got to stick together, Mickey, right?"

"Yup. Gotta watch each other's backs." And thank God Eli had a strong enough back to help with the jobs outside the fort, of which there had been more than Danner had anticipated, since they'd still not fully filled their need for drivers.

That night, after walking the forty-minute round trip to Rosie's Diner, Maggie headed up to the Huntington's grand home, which they called a cottage. She stood on the front step for a moment, then decided she should go to the back door. But they had no servants to answer back there, not unless they'd hired someone. The front door opened. Jesse Huntington's broad smile quickly vanished as he surveyed her from head to toe. He stepped outside and closed the door behind him.

"What are you doing here?" He crossed his arms. "And why are you dressing up and passing yourself off as one of your brothers?"

Ire rose up in her. "You owe my family money," she blurted out.

His face registered shock at her words and then shame. "But you needn't come up here. You could have sent another bill."

"Yet another bill?" She scowled at him. "I sent you plenty last winter that went unanswered."

A muscle in his jaw twitched. "We'll take care of that soon."

She nodded, looking down at her scuffed brown boots. Why did the man have to look so blasted handsome even when he was being difficult? "That's not why I'm here. I'm here about the driver position." *About the housing that went with it.*

"What on earth do you mean?"

She raised her head and returned his steady gaze. "Your sister, Vivienne, said you need a driver."

"Vivienne?"

"Yes." Since he apparently didn't know about what was going on, Maggie wasn't about to discuss this further with him. "Can you please get her?"

"A driver," he muttered under his breath, "is just what we don't need." He whirled around and opened the door. The scent of burnt ham carried out. Maggie cringed.

The door reopened and both the blonde and brunette sisters appeared.

"Oh this is just delicious. We'll have a driver again." The younger girl extended a dainty hand. "I'm Vivienne."

The other young woman nodded gravely and then thrust out her hand. "Florence Huntington."

"Pleased to meet ya both. I'm Mickey Hadley."

"You were our driver when we arrived." Vivienne's squinted up at her and Maggie averted her gaze.

"Yes'm."

"Vivie needs rides to and from town at night, as may our mother, and we'll need a driver once our own horses arrive on the island." Florence's clipped voice was as different from her mother's genteel Southern drawl as was possible.

Maggie turned toward the elder sister but kept her head lowered slightly. "And when will that be? For the horses?"

"In fact, your father Mr. Hadley sent us a letter saying they were being shipped this weekend and Mr. Danner would help send them up." Florence tapped her black boot to emphasize her words.

Vivienne edged slightly forward. "Your father actually suggested we contact you, Mickey, to see if you might be interested in our arrangement. But I'd hoped my dear bosom friend Abigail would have her husband drive for us at night."

Florence huffed a laugh. "But we can't afford to pay Eli, and the Mitchells already have lodgings and meals with the Wellings." Florence's no-nonsense tone continued to perplex Maggie. Weren't Southern women supposedly more docile?

"Yes, you're quite right, Florence." The pretty blonde girl's dulcet tones clashed with that of her sister's.

"If you're interested, Mr. Hadley, follow me and I'll show you the carriage house." Florence bustled past her and Maggie turned and followed.

Vivienne linked her arm through Maggie's and leaned in. "Now I don't mind telling you that none of us Huntingtons is much of a cook, but we're trying our best. And Florence has become a proficient fisherwoman."

She couldn't keep her eyebrows from shooting up. "Really? Because I'm pretty handy with a skillet."

Vivienne leaned in. "I'm quite sure you are, *Miss* Hadley."

Maggie turned and stared at the girl beside her, who had raised a finger to her pursed lips. "How did you know?" She'd have to fix it. Work harder.

"Oh, pooh." Vivienne tossed a blonde curl over her slim shoulder. "I got to thinking about what your brother, Russell, used to tell me."

Florence turned and scowled. "You had no business running around with him last summer."

Vivienne giggled. "But we had so much fun. It was invigorating to be free of Jesse's tyranny."

"A slight exaggeration. Our brother isn't a tyrant. He's more of a—"

"Bully." Vivienne pouted.

Florence made a guttural sound. "He's no more a bully than I am."

When Vivienne rolled her eyes upward, Maggie couldn't restrain her giggle. She liked these two Huntington women.

"All right, he's not a bully or a tyrant but he always thinks he knows best."

"Because he's usually right, when it comes to you." Florence pulled a set of keys from her reticule.

Shrugging, Vivienne withdrew her arm from Maggie's. She pointed to the two-carriages-wide and two-stories-tall carriage house. "What would interest you in driving for us?"

Maggie rubbed her eyes. "Being able to sleep at night, and breathe, might be two good reasons."

"What do you mean?" Vivienne cocked her head.

"My room is in the barn. And even though I am in our Percherons' barn plenty at home, I don't sleep there."

"Of course you do not." Florence nodded firmly. "This will work out perfectly for all of us."

"I'll help you look a little more manly." Vivienne placed her tiny hands on either side of Maggie's face. "And I can help you with a bit of theatrical makeup."

"Really?" That could be good.

"Yes!" The girl dropped her hands and clapped. "This could be so much fun having Russell's sister right here with us."

Florence caught Maggie's eye. "You cook up the fish I catch and teach me some more basic cooking skills and I'll be very grateful. The books I've read don't adequately explain the techniques."

Vivienne shrugged. "We eat a lot of burnt food."

This seemed too good an opportunity to be true. "What's the catch?"

"If our brother figures out that you're a woman, he'll likely ensure that you have absolutely no opportunity for fun." Vivienne's perfect lips formed a pout.

"Absolutely no fun?" Florence's droll repetition as a question, was followed by her leading them up the stairs to the second-floor entrance. "If one would like to put oneself at constant risk and considers that fun, then Vivienne is correct. However, some of us can find joy in the simple things."

Vivienne sighed as Florence unlocked the door. "Jesse always makes sure we don't get into what he calls 'mischief'."

"Until he was working with Father last summer." Florence turned and wagged a finger at her sister. "And now I have to say I don't blame Jesse for watching us, or rather you, so closely."

Cheeks pink, Vivienne ducked past Florence into the long spacious room.

"Your brother already knows I'm Maggie Hadley." She removed her hat, her now-short hair brushing her shoulders.

"He knows?" Vivienne gaped at her.

Florence pulled a white sheet from a blue upholstered chair that looked far too pretty for a carriage house. "How?"

"I met your father and brother at our Percheron farm in Pickford last year, when he purchased two of our horses."

"Aha." Florence and Vivienne exchanged a knowing look.

"Aha, what?"

"Did he speak with you?" Florence's tone was judge-like solemn.

"Briefly."

Vivienne giggled. "No wonder he wanted to personally go to your parents' farm when we got up here."

Had he truly wanted to come to Pickford? "To settle the bill, I'm sure."

Florence crossed her arms. "Humph."

Was that footfall Maggie heard on the stairs?

"No wonder he's always asking us if we've seen our driver around town." Vivienne practically bounced in her cream-colored pumps. "Oh, romance is in the air. It surely must be."

Flummoxed, Maggie could only stare, open-mouthed. This kind of thinking had to be stopped. "As long as there's no hay dust floating around up here, I think that's what will matter."

Jesse popped his head around the doorframe. "What's in the air?"

Sun pierced the Irish lace curtains in Jesse's east-facing window. Although he had a beautiful view of the harbor, this room also afforded the earliest sunlight in the morning. He tossed back the brocade coverings on his bed and rose. His bare feet connected with the wool latch hook rug and he smiled at the soft touch of it. Florence had already started going through the house cataloging all the items. At least his rug would stay as she felt it couldn't bring much if sold.

He donned his robe and tied the belt at his waist then he slid his feet into his expensive leather slippers—another item Flo couldn't sell off.

At least he slept better at night knowing that Maggie Hadley was safely ensconced in the carriage house. One less worry—although having her so near had prompted him to spend more time in the evenings checking on her. She, his sisters, and even his mother had also enjoyed a rousing game of Pinochle and had taken tea together after church on Sunday.

He descended the stairs and stopped at the landing. His mother's image reflected in the mirror on the oak hall tree. She draped a silky-looking black shawl over her crisp white pintucked blouse. A large cameo perched at the top of Mother's blouse. With that stark black shawl around her narrow shoulders, she looked almost. . . frightening. Her pale skin, ebony hair streaked with silver, and lips lightly rouged made her resemble a ghoul. Jesse shivered.

"Mother, where did you get that ghastly shawl?" He completed his descent down the stairs.

She whirled away from the mirror and arched one dark brow. "You should thank me to wear this."

He shoved his hands into his robe's deep pockets. "And why would that be?"

Florence peeked around the corner, clutching a biscuit in her hand. "She's cozying up to Mrs. Nouri."

"Ah." *Poor dear mother.* "You're willing to dress like the superintendent's mother if it helps my cause?"

She wagged her index finger at him. "You'll see. I've found a way to get you that job."

Not one word from the school board yet, after a week. But connections could be everything as he well knew. "And how will that be?"

Florence guffawed, then covered her mouth with her free hand.

Mother glared at his sister. "Remember what you promised me, Florence Catherine."

His sister gestured as though she were locking her lips tight and then throwing away the key. She spun on her heel and headed toward the back of the house, presumably for breakfast.

"Did you already eat, Mother?"

"I'm not hungry." She turned away from him and back toward the mirror.

He was grateful she hadn't caught his disapproving glare. He schooled his features back into a placid expression. Mother wasn't eating still, here on the island. His younger sister had taken in most of her garments. Vivienne was accustomed to working on costumes for theatrical productions and those skills came in handy now.

"I'm going out," Mother announced.

"But we don't have a driver until Mickey returns."

She sniffed. "I have a friend coming for me on the half hour."

"Who is this friend?" Was his mother already being courted, despite being in mourning?

"A lady friend, if it is any of your business, which it is not." Apparently Flo's demeanor was rubbing off a little on Mother.

Jesse pressed a hand to his chest. "My apologies."

She nodded curtly. "Accepted." Lips pinched tightly together, she went to the door and stared out the glass panes. Then she swiveled toward him. "I'll also be going out this evening. On my own. So the carriage will be in use, and I'll have Mickey wait on me."

What is Mother up to? A niggling sense of unease worked though him.

"June is fast escaping us, and Independence Day will soon be celebrated. So if you're working for Mr. Danner all day and you drive for us at night and on weekends, when will you have any fun?" Vivienne Huntington fixed Maggie with an accusatory stare as she, her sister, and Maggie sat in chairs outside, in the back yard, which surprisingly wasn't as overgrown as one would expect.

Maggie shrugged. "It's what I have to do." She had to keep income coming in, to help her family.

Florence's nose twitched. "A lot of people around here are having to do what they have to do to survive." She peeled potatoes while Vivienne stitched repairs in an off-white muslin gown.

Vivienne tied off a knot in the lace and muslin dress's shoulder, then cut the thread. "There! No one would ever know."

Maggie stopped polishing the leather straps and leaned in, as a breeze wafted the scent of nearby roses toward them. Roses did not trim themselves. There were no servants here, according to the Huntington sisters. When Vivienne flipped

65

the fabric to its right side, Maggie leaned closer. "I can't see anything wrong."

A wide smile lit up Vivienne's pretty face. "And when we all go up to the Independence Day party at the fort, no one will see anything wrong with our friend, Margaret, who will be accompanying us."

Maggie stiffened, then shook her head. "No. Nope. Can't do that." For one thing, if Mauvais was there, he might recognize her. "I can't have anyone guessing."

Vivie laughed. "You must think me an amateur."

Blinking, Maggie tried to cover her insult, "No, of course not, I know you've been in many theatrical productions."

Snorting, Florence ran her fingers over the garment. "It's a fine muslin, but of course not something we Huntingtons would be seen in. But our dear friend, from Charleston, who is in reduced circumstances, would be perfectly appropriate. Doesn't even require a hat. Nor gloves."

"Good thing she wears gloves when she drives— because that could be a 'tell' of her being a laborer." Vivie's cheeks pinked. "No offense meant, Maggie."

Maggie lifted her palm. "None taken. It's what I do. But I can't don a dress and take the chance of being recognized."

"An umbrella!" Florence proclaimed. "If she keeps that open some of the time, or has a fan, that surely would help."

"Her face is usually covered by a handkerchief and her hair by that ugly hat."

"My hair is short now."

"Not too short to pin up, twist, and curl." Vivienne cocked her head as she raised the dress and held it beneath Maggie's chin.

"Makeup around her eyes, just a touch, would make her look different. And something on her brows."

"Yes!" Vivienne whooped. "Now we can have some fun."

They'd worn her down. "Only on one condition. Sergeant Mauvais can't be there."

"I can find out." Florence set the bowl of potatoes and peelings aside. "I'll ask around when I bring some cigars up there to sell."

"What?" Maggie gaped.

Florence batted her eyelashes innocently. "If you have any arguments about Vivie's ability to transform someone, then let me ask you this—who did you think I was yesterday, when I asked you if you'd like to buy one of my very fine cigars?"

Maggie forced her mouth closed. A young gent, mid to late twenties, with a sad-looking beard, wearing a mustard and purple plaid old fashioned suit, had approached them at the fort's gate. She'd shaken her head at the salesman, but Eli had insisted the man jump up on the back of the dray, and he had. Only that wasn't a *he*, but a she. "I heard, when they unloaded, that most of those soldiers wanted the luxury of a fine cigar at a price much better than in town."

Pretending to pull at nonexistent suit lapels, Florence dropped her voice, "Our excellent brand is the best around."

Vivie giggled as Maggie pointed at Florence. "You make one ugly looking man."

"So they aren't threatened by me at all." Florence quirked her eyebrows. "I'll grab some more of Dad's hidden cigars and bring them up there. If Mauvais is going to be there, we could form some kind of protective circle around you. Jesse will be with us."

"Jesse?" As much as she feared being recognized as a female, wouldn't it be nice to have Jesse Huntington see her once again in a more feminine state?

"He won't let the sergeant get anywhere near our special guest."

Some of Jesse's stress had dissipated the previous day, when he'd cashed out some emergency money that his father had remaining at the Mackinac Island Savings Bank. He'd immediately written and sent payment to Mr. Hadley. Now as he accompanied Maggie and his sisters into the fort, for the Independence Day celebration, he didn't feel as weighed down as he'd been.

Outside the back of the fort a brass band played a jaunty tune that made Jesse's spirits lift even higher—that and having Maggie Hadley on his arm. Their "guest" was attired in a simple, but pretty, white muslin gown that Vivie had worn in one of her productions—playing a struggling young maid who aspired for something more in life.

What did Maggie aspire to? She, like he, wished to help provide for family members. But did she want more? Mr. Hadley had implied that his daughter would be the best one to run his horse farm once he no longer could do so. Was that her genuine wish? She certainly had a way with those mighty Percherons.

"You look deep in thought, Mr. Huntington." Maggie actually batted her eyelashes at him.

He almost laughed. "Yes, well, I give you leave to call me Jesse, dear Margaret."

She dipped her head, almost coquettishly. Was this all an act, or was there anything in her behavior which expressed a female interest in him?

Even if she did, he wasn't in a situation to provide for her or any woman—he had three ladies he had to support.

Maggie opened her lacy fan and waved it in front of her face as they entered through the open gates of the fort. Inside, red-white-and-blue buntings and banners hung from the porch rails by the officers' quarters and other buildings which ringed the compound.

Some soldiers strolled the wooden walkways in the back.

Florence pointed forward. "Let's go to where the luncheon is set up."

He suppressed a laugh. Ever since Flo had heard there was smoked whitefish, trout, and perch being served, his fish-loving sister rejoiced that she wouldn't have to catch them—but could simply enjoy the freshwater fish. "Certainly. Lead on."

After all, Florence, it turned out, had a steady business with the soldiers disposing of father's cigar supply. Today, though, she was attired in an expensive Worth summer gown, last season's of course, but still fashionable. Her upswept hair was topped by a perky hat that matched the gown's multiple shades of burgundy and green.

"Hey! Hey Mr. Jesse!" Jack Welling, attired in a navy and white sailor suit sprinted toward them.

He pulled Maggie closer.

"Hello Jack."

His sisters, as they had planned, stepped between the boy and Jesse and Maggie. The two fussed and fawned over the boy.

Jack waved their hands away as Florence and Vivie both tried to touch his sailor outfit. "Get off, you two! I want to talk to Jesse."

"He's busy escorting our dear friend. So let him be." Flo's stern voice would have stopped most kids in their tracks.

Jack pushed past Flo and Vivie. "Hey, look what my folks made me wear!" He crinkled his nose in disgust. "Makes me want to—" he stuck his fingers into his mouth.

"That's enough!" Jesse wheeled Maggie away. "That's not appropriate talk around ladies."

"Oh! Sorry Miss!" Jack blinked up at Maggie, who was fanning herself vigorously.

She dipped her chin.

Jack poked him on his shoulder. "Did you get yourself a gal, Mr. Jesse?"

"Go on away now and play your part in the drama, Jack." Vivie pointed to where a half-dozen children had gathered, all attired in military-style clothing.

Flo raised her skirts slightly and pushed past them. "I'm going to the food, and I suggest you follow."

Maggie cast him an amused glance and laughed. "I guess we're going to partake of refreshments, now, Mr. Huntington."

"She looks like a major general, charging through the people ahead of us." Vivie squared her shoulders. "Makes me proud."

Jesse closed his eyes hard for a moment. "God help us all."

"Oh He will help us, if we but ask His mercies every day." Maggie assumed a slight Southern accent infused with piety.

Vivie's eyes widened. "We could use you in our Thanksgiving production, Mag. . . Margaret."

"For what part?"

"A nun from Savannah who has escaped from being imprisoned by the Yankees—"

Jesse raised his hand. "Better watch what you're saying and doing in these parts. You're not in the South anymore."

"And the only acting I'm intending to do is as a dray driver," Maggie muttered.

"Suit yourself. But you'd get rave reviews from your audience." Vivie picked up her pace. "Flo was supposed to stay right with us and help form our human shield."

Jesse and Maggie hurried to keep up with Vivie, who was closing in on Flo.

How strange to have Maggie Hadley on his arm, looking fresh as a daisy—and loveliness itself. The purity of her ensemble suited her. The faint sadness in her eyes did not.

Soon they partook in selecting from the food all set out on multiple large tables covered in simple canvas throws. Each carried their plate to a nearby small table surrounded by rustic pine chairs.

He took a drink of the lemonade that one of the soldiers had poured for them. "Are you enjoying yourself, Margaret?"

"I am enjoying the display on the field." She pointed to the parade grounds where the soldiers were performing drills. "And the food and company are excellent."

"Agreed." Florence raised her lemonade glass and Vivie and he did the same.

"We should do this more often."

"It took hours for your sisters to transform me." Maggie shook her head slowly. "I'm afraid this is my one day to shine."

As if in agreement, sunshine streamed through the clouds.

"We enjoy our dray driver's company, too." He winked at her.

She blushed.

What would it be like to be able to attend social engagements with Maggie—"all dressed up" as his sisters put it—on a regular basis?

He may never know. She'd need to return to the mainland before winter and he'd need to continue searching for employment that could support his family.

When the tides turned for the two of them, would they be separated—permanently?

Chapter Six

Late July

The Huntington women were definitely up to something, Maggie sensed it, but she didn't want to push them for their confidences. Since their special fourth of July outing, two weeks earlier, Florence shared, over fish fry that Maggie had cooked, that the cigars were all gone and she was cataloging items in the attic. But she never divulged what she planned to do. Vivienne waved at Maggie, in the driver's seat, as the young woman exited the carriage. Goldy and Silver snorted their annoyance at being parked by the curb. They'd already gotten used to taking a nice quick ride from the West Bluff through Hubbard's Annex and the pair wasn't keen on going back to town. On the nearby walkway, Vivienne clutched her reticule to her chest as she hurried toward the Christy Tea Shoppe.

Earlier that day, Maggie spied Florence toting a tin pail of goods into town. It really wasn't Maggie's business, but what had Florence traded, in order to procure some baked goods for her family? And did her brother know?

Four boys raced down the main street, hooting and hollering as they went but the Huntington's horses didn't react. Passersby on the walkway by Lake Huron gawked at the boys. Funny how horses could be so ornery about some things yet so lackadaisical about others—like some people were. Goldy and Silver had always been a little different from the other Percherons at the Hadley stables.

Vivienne soon returned to the curb, hoisting up a small but bulging bag. "My mother will love these almond buttercream cookies. They're her favorites." Moisture gleamed in her eyes.

Trying to conceal her concern over Vivienne's distress, Maggie dipped her chin and lowered her voice. "Best get in the carriage, Miss, and let's be on our way."

"Oh, Mickey, I'm so worried about my mother. She's not been herself since we've been here." Vivienne burst into tears and then swooped into the carriage.

The carriage rocked only slightly as Vivienne settled herself. After checking traffic, Maggie directed Goldy and Silver onto the road again. When they reached the Huntington's home, Jesse's mother, attired in black from head-to-toe, stood expectantly beneath a tall oak tree that edged the drive. Maggie frowned.

Mrs. Huntington waved to her. "Don't unhitch the horses, I have a social engagement."

Vivienne disembarked and went to her mother and gave her a quick hug. "I brought your favorite cookies. See?" She opened the bag.

"Soon we won't have to live on a pittance." Mrs. Huntington's pointy chin tipped upward. She squared her shoulders beneath what had to have been the most hideous black silk shawl ever made. Even a country woman such as Maggie's mother wouldn't have been seen in such a covering. And what had come about, that the woman believed their finances were about to improve? Had Jesse landed a job in the city? He'd continued to send out applications, he'd said, with no success.

The woman, looking like a spectral apparition, with all her black clothing floating around her, approached the front of the carriage. "Young man, you'll take me to Mrs. Nouri's home in town."

Maggie stiffened. Mr. Danner had specifically instructed her to stay away from the woman and her home. Her boss would be upset if he heard she had. But she wasn't driving his dray—she was driving the Huntington's carriage. "Are you sure, ma'am?"

She cringed as the woman shot her a scathing glance. "Did I not just say so?" Then she appeared to draw in a slow breath. "My deah young mahn, I will not issue you an order that I am unsure of." Her heavy Southern accent was back in full force.

"Yes, ma'am. Do you need help into the carriage, ma'am?"

"No, thank you. I can manage." Mrs. Huntington sniffed and then climbed into the carriage, slamming the door behind her in a fashion that could not possibly be construed as evidence of a Southern Belle with genteel upbringing.

Maggie exhaled a long breath and then directed the team to circle out of the drive and back down toward the road.

As they approached the small clapboard house which sat a street back on Market Street, a number of elderly women approached it. Wrapped in similar black shawls, all wore black or dark skirts some with matching shirtwaists. Some sported black arm bands. Unease worked its way through her hands and the horses must have noticed, because they wandered, and she had to bring them back under control. Maybe she should turn around.

A sharp thump from within the carriage alerted her as they neared the small house, her employer's sign to stop. Maggie pulled the carriage next to the curb.

Mrs. Huntington exited and stepped onto the sidewalk. She turned and pointed her finger at Maggie. "Now, not a word, young man."

A stout woman, the butcher's wife if Maggie recollected correctly, hurried alongside Jesse's mother. "Mrs. Huntington, it's so wonderful that you could come."

Mrs. Huntington, cheeks flushed, turned from Maggie and toward the other woman.

The unease Maggie experienced built more strongly as the two women strode toward Mrs. Nouri's house.

She flicked her reins and the Percherons moved on. Without barely thinking of where she was going, Maggie soon found herself at Reverend McWithey's manse near the church. If ever she needed some spiritual advice, it was now.

Why me, Lord? Jesse's first conversation with God in a long while seemed so short. And since he'd lost his father and almost everything of worldly value in his life it seemed strange he'd not asked the question earlier. Maybe because he wasn't sure God could be trusted with matters which men could fix themselves—by putting more effort into something. Father had taught him that. But Father was wrong. Jesse's only job prospect required him to yank his mother from the school superintendent's mother's home. *I need help from a power greater than myself.*

Maggie had dropped his mother off earlier and then spoken with their preacher. She'd returned to their cottage and shared what Rev. McWithey had told her. Although Jesse wouldn't make a scene extricating his mother, he had no intention of allowing her to participate in a séance at Mrs. Nouri's. Father would be rolling over in his grave if he knew what Mother was up to.

Jesse stepped onto the walkway and waved at Maggie, seated in the driver's seat of the carriage, as he headed off. Hard to believe numerous wealthy ladies, many from fine families, all sharing some tragic loss, were gathered at the superintendent's mother's home. Ahead, although the sun was only now setting, and twilight cast a golden glow, the Nouri's heavy curtains were fully shut which shouldn't have surprised Jesse. Vivienne had argued with him and Maggie that perhaps Mother was simply researching for a play that the community would be doing in the autumn, a theatrical production in which someone died during a phony séance. That wasn't likely Mother's goal. Especially not when Florence finally admitted to them that Mother wouldn't allow her to box up Father's personal jewelry for keeping because she intended to "use them" herself. Flo had learned that Mother was bringing them to Mrs. Nouri's home with the intention of conjuring up a connection with Father.

He shivered.

But he'd not really thought out his plan. What if Mrs. Nouri's servants wouldn't let him in?

Jesse scanned the street. Most of the tourists were in for the night or heading toward their hotels. Workers were already in bed, ready to wake at the crack of dawn since they were still in high season and grateful for a job. Carefully, Jesse crossed the street and then approached Mrs. Nouri's two-story home. Even in this light he could see that the building could use a coat of paint. And weeds sprung up all over the front yard. Why did the superintendent not help her keep the property up? Furthermore, why did he allow his mother to run séances in her home?

Candlelight or lamps flickered behind the dark curtains as Jesse walked around to the side of the home. Scruffy shrubs hugged the home alongside and as he approached the back. A narrow, covered entryway door centered the back of the structure. He continued around to the other side. Strangely, on the west side of the home there was yet another narrow doorway. He sensed movement from the detached one-deep carriage house in the back and hurried around to the front.

He mounted the three stairs to the oak door and brought the brass knocker down once, twice, three times.

An ebony-skinned manservant, attired in a gold-embroidered satin vest and dark breeches opened the door. "No men admitted tonight, sir."

When the servant attempted to close the door on him, Jesse shoved his foot inside the door and pushed forward into the entryway. The servant, more slightly built, stepped back, eyes wide.

"I'm looking for my mother, Mrs. Huntington."

The man splayed his white-gloved hands. "No names here, sir."

No names. Well that figured. Because even though such behavior might be considered in vogue among the Victorian elite, among many other conservative church-going folks, such as those who primarily populated this island, trying to contact the dead would be frowned upon.

"Where are they?" Jesse practically growled. He wasn't about to have his mother engage in this behavior, neither would he have her squander what funds they did have. Fully half of the cash he'd hidden in Father's cigar box was gone and he believed his sisters when they denied taking it. And certainly Maggie hadn't. He'd not even asked her. Didn't need to. When she'd come to him and shared about what his mother was about to do, a little part of his heart went to her in payment.

She understood him, understood his heart, and she'd done him a favor he'd need to repay.

"Please, sir, I can't lose my job."

Jesse understood the pleading in the man's voice. "Help me get in there, then, and get my mother out of there."

"Wait here, sir. Let me tell her there be an emergency at her home."

"All right. But make it quick." Jesse fingered the gold watch in his vest. How much longer would he be able to keep his timepiece?

End of season at best.

In a few moments, his mother joined him in the entryway, the scent of incense clinging to her clothing. "What's wrong, Jesse?" But guilt, more than concern, etched her features.

"Come along, Mother." He frowned at her in warning. "I'll tell you later."

Once outside the building he intended to give her a piece of his mind. But she was his mother. On the other hand. . .

She reached into her burgundy velvet reticule and retrieved an envelope full of cash. "I'm sorry. I should have asked. But I was so desperate to ask your Papa about what we should do that—"

Nearby a door creaked open. "Shh!" Jesse touched his mother's shoulder. "Let's watch," he whispered. He pointed to the side of the house. He took her hand and led her to the corner. He ducked his head around in time to see a slim man, attired all in black, enter. Mother looked, too, just as the door closed. This must be the human who would project a ghostlike voice to answer attendee's questions from the great beyond.

"Oh," she breathed the word on a disappointed sigh. "I can guess what that's all about. I'm not so daft as to not know I was about to be duped."

"It's all right, Mother." Jesse patted her hand. "But please don't do that again."

"I promise. But oh dear, Jesse, what now about the job?"

"What about it?"

"The superintendent's mother was going to put in a good word for you, but with me leaving the meeting I wonder if she will." Mother pushed a strand of hair back from her brow. "Was my payment for reaching your father akin to buying a favor from her son?"

Jesse shook his head. "If the superintendent is in on this nonsense then I don't want anything to do with him."

But with few choices left on the island for work, what could he do?

The gold watch would go sooner than later.

Having been summoned by the superintendent for an interview that very afternoon, Jesse spent some time with his grooming. He'd need a haircut and a shave. But why was he bothering? This entire situation with the man's mother had almost put Jesse off the notion of trying his hand at teaching. Séances at his own mother's home?

Soon, Jesse was settled in the barber's chair. He'd need to go home to change into his suit afterward. He removed his spectacles and tucked them in his pocket. The barber sharpened his straight razor on the long leather strop alongside the chair. "I hear you're interviewing for the teacher's job."

"Yes, sir."

"Shame that James Baker had to cancel his contract at the last minute."

"Oh?"

"Good thing you're here."

The scent of lime hung thick in the air. A boy of not more than twelve swept up the hair clippings from the floor.

"But aren't you Huntington's son?"

Oh no, here started the fishing expedition wherein the locals would try to learn Jesse's personal business. "Could be. What if I am?"

"No need to get worried. You wouldn't be the first boy from those cliffs to have to join those of us down in the village."

How low the high and mighty could become. Was that what he meant? "Simply cut my hair and give me a good shave and I'll be happy." And he'd give him a good tip if he stopped talking.

Later, as he sat in the interview chair, a black Windsor with a spindle back that dug into his spine, Jesse wished he'd allowed the barber to practice his interrogation skills on him. With his terse manner and narrow beady eyes, Mr. Nouri continued to ask Jesse about his schooling, his work history, and why he wanted the job.

About to lose his patience, Jesse shoved his glasses to the bridge of his nose. "Sir, it seems to me that perhaps you don't wish to hire me."

Nouri's dark brows knit together. "I may have reason."

Reason? What reason could he possibly have? Jesse sat at the edge of his seat and cocked his head. "Sir?"

"You were seen coming from my mother's home last night."

Jesse's lips involuntarily pursed. "Yes, sir. I was taking my mother home from there."

"Oh?" Nouri's shoulders flexed beneath his tightly cut dark wool suit. "My mother felt you'd been discourteous to her manservant."

Tension rippled up his spine. "Sir, you've asked me a great many questions. May I ask you one?"

He shrugged. "Why not?"

Leaning forward, he fixed his gaze on the older man, as his father would often do in a business deal. "Do you condone your mother's behavior?"

"Her behavior? Whatever do you mean?"

"These séances she holds in her home. That's what I mean. Wherein older women, widows like my mother, pay exorbitant fees to contact their loved ones." A muscle twitched in his jaw.

"What?" The man shot to his feet so fast that a small crystal paperweight globe on his wide walnut desk rolled off toward Jesse, who caught it. "How dare you make such accusations, young man."

Face hot, Jesse slowly rose. "It's true, sir."

The man sputtered but then turned away from Jesse to face the windows behind him.

Should he go or stay? Something pinned Jesse to the spot. If Mr. Nouri didn't know about his mother perhaps it was high time he did. When the man still said nothing, Jesse placed the crystal orb back on the desk. "Superintendent Nouri, I know what I had to do with my own mother. If you feel the same as I do about such things, you'll surely speak to your mother and set her straight. In a respectful way, of course, sir."

Nouri said nothing.

"I'll see myself out, sir."

"Wait." The man swiveled around and fixed Jesse with a surprisingly understanding look. "I'll get my mother in hand, and you keep yours above reproach as well, and we'll get along fine."

"Yes, sir."

"Sit down. Let me tell you about your duties and the pay and what not." Nouri ran a hand through his dark hair and lowered himself to his seat again.

Really? He had the job? And he'd gotten it by speaking honestly. Memories of his father jumped to mind. Father had been frank and clear in his business dealings. He'd never cheated anyone, and he'd regretted terribly all those who'd been affected when his businesses failed. He was gruff but fair. But could the same be said of his cronies? Did his fellow businessmen speak honestly when they denied that they owed his father any debt of obligation? Maybe Florence was right.

Let the books speak for themselves.

Chapter Seven

If Jesse's two sisters weren't with them on this picnic, Maggie would have found the outing almost romantic. On her free day, after church, all four of them had ridden bikes out to Arch Rock. Mrs. Welling had loaned them the bikes and had cautioned her son, Jack, that he couldn't join them—she had chores for him.

Florence spread out a moth-eaten pink wool blanket on the ground. They had both an excellent view of Lake Huron and the limestone arch formation high on the hillside. Jesse plopped down and spread himself out on the blanket. He pulled his straw boater hat over his face and feigned snoring. Vivienne laughed and plucked his hat off his handsome face.

Maggie shook her head. She retrieved the picnic basket from the bike. "If you don't work, you don't eat is what my ma always says."

Florence huffed. "Jesse will starve then, because he didn't buy, prepare, or transport any of these items."

He jumped up and strode to Maggie. "I believe you ladies will have to eat your words."

Vivienne rolled her eyes. "Why is that?"

His warm fingers brushed against Maggie's, sending a thrill through her. He took the woven-wood basket and lifted the lid's left side. "What do you see in there?"

Maggie peered inside and then removed the wax paper covering a deep square tin. Thick sandwiches were stacked high. She daintily lifted the thick bread on the top one. "Tomatoes even? And is that ham?"

She looked up and caught his eye.

He was beaming. "Yes, indeed."

Vivienne rushed forward and opened the basket's other side and peeked in. "Apple salad? Oh, is that German salad, too?"

Florence joined them and reached into the middle section. She pulled out a bag and opened it and looked inside. She sniffed appreciatively. "Those are Mrs. Christy's chocolate pecan bars, I'm sure."

"You're right." Jesse waggled his eyebrows. "And your friend Abigail can indeed keep a secret, Vivie."

"From me?" Vivienne feigned a pout.

Florence poked him. "You must have gotten an early paycheck."

"I did. Although it's only the beginning of September, and school won't begin until later in the month, Mr. Nouri surprised me with an advance."

"Hurrah." Florence pretended to wave a flag.

Jesse pushed her hand down. "You mocked me for *not* working to make this picnic happen, but I did all I could to make it a fun surprise."

Maggie wanted to hug his neck. He'd even kept the secret from her. Their eyes met, her cheeks heating when they'd held the gaze a bit too long.

Florence brushed her hands together. "Then what did you do with the picnic we had put together?"

With Maggie working all week and driving Vivienne back and forth to theater practice each night, she'd not had much chance to help the sisters with cooking. Florence had learned to make a passable chicken salad sandwich from tinned meat and mayonnaise. The soldiers had given Maggie a few items from the fort's garden. And Vivienne had baked two loaves of wheat bread that had not quite fully risen. That was to have been their picnic. *Thankfully not.*

Jesse brought the picnic basket to the blanket's edge and set it down. "Abigail was going to pick ours up and deliver it to the Oakford family, who took in those orphans."

"That was awful news about the horrid fire in Minnesota." Vivienne's eyes misted over.

Maggie blinked back her own tears. She'd read about the devastation in one of the papers left at the stables. "I don't think the residents of Hinckley will ever recover from that tragedy." How horrible to have a conflagration destroy their town.

"The Oakford's nieces will be in my classroom when we start, but Mrs. Oakford says they barely speak." Jesse sat down on the blanket. "I think I'm in for more than I bargained for."

"Things happen, though." Maggie didn't mean to blurt out her comment. Surely these three Huntington siblings knew exactly how quickly life could change.

As if in agreement, a breeze stirred the leaves on the ground, some already golden-hued. The leaves whirled around them for a moment before settling again. All four of them remained quiet and a pensive solemnity cloaked them as Maggie settled on the blanket.

Florence kicked off her sturdy black shoes and sat beside Maggie, tucking her skirts around her. "We won't be able to do this much longer." The way she said the words, implied she wasn't really speaking about the autumn weather. Maggie was intrigued by her tone and comment, but Jesse and Vivienne looked nonplussed.

Vivienne slowly lowered herself onto the blanket, arranging her skirts around her.

Jesse passed out tin plates, napkins, and utensils. "I'll say the blessing."

Maggie couldn't keep her eyes from widening. She'd been praying that Jesse might show more interest in God's direction, as he never voiced any. Maggie had been the one to say prayers at meals at the Huntingtons' long cherry dining table.

"Lord, for all you have given us, may we truly be thankful. For the work you have offered and that which you have prepared for us to do, may you enable us. May we be thankful for this food you have provided. In Jesus's name, Amen."

When Maggie opened her eyes, Jesse opened his, too, and looked directly at her. A thrill skipped through her heart.

Even if nothing ever became of their friendship, and how could it, still she would treasure the progress her new friend was making with God in his life.

If Maggie Hadley had been attired in a gauzy teatime gown and glittering with jewels, as the young ladies at the Grand Hotel often were, she couldn't have looked more appealing. Beneath her broad-brimmed straw hat, summer had brought a glow to her complexion and freckled her pert nose. Her bright eyes and perfectly shaped lips urged him to move closer to her on the blanket. But with his two sisters watching, and Maggie passing as a lad, any such movement would be unthinkable.

He reached over, grabbed a cluster of grapes and popped one in his mouth, then reclined back. "Guess who I am, Vivienne."

"That's easy." Vivienne grabbed the grapes from him. "You're Julius Caesar, from our plays."

"No, I'm being Christopher Oakford who plays the part of Caesar." He winked at Maggie, and she blushed.

Vivienne swatted at him, and he leaned away. "That makes no sense. Christopher is acting as Caesar and therefor you were acting as if you were Caesar not as Mr. Oakford."

"Nope." He reached for more grapes and Maggie leaned in, broke off a cluster, and handed them to him, smiling.

Florence gave him one of her imperious looks. She'd pull off a better "teacher face" than he'd manage. "Don't expect Jesse to make sense. His arguments are often circular."

All three women laughed.

"I don't argue. I persuade." He raised his eyebrows.

"How about when I told you I wished to take a ferry to St. Ignace?" Vivienne smirked.

"That's different. You never would specify exactly why you needed to go." In fact, she'd not even made up a reason that he might have approved.

"I wanted to see a friend. And I'm almost eighteen. I ought to be able to keep some things to myself, like Flo does."

Florence gave their sister a quelling look, her features flashing a warning. "If your friend was a respectable person, then you'd have no hesitation in telling Jesse."

Maggie waved her hand. "Please, let's enjoy our lunch. I only have the one free day."

"Sorry, Maggie." And he was. He didn't wish to upset her. "Let's take a walk after we eat."

If he had his way, he'd take her hand and walk with her. But how would that look? They'd both be run off the island. Either that, or Maggie would have to reveal her true identity and give up her job.

"I brought my harmonica." Maggie beamed.

"Did Eli finally teach you that last Stephen Foster song?" Vivienne took a bite of salad.

"He did."

They finished their lunch and strolled along Lake Huron. Each Huntington shared a little bit more about themselves than Maggie had previously known. Florence had completed a bookkeeping course over the summer, by correspondence. Vivienne was asked to join a traveling theatrical troupe but had refused. And Jesse had purchased some books on best education practices and had read through most of them.

"I can't say that I agree with some of the methods that our modern teachers use." Jesse bent and picked up a maple leaf tinged with yellow, red, and orange. "This one's a beauty, isn't it?" He passed the leaf to Maggie and she accepted it, painfully aware of his sister's wide eyes.

"We're fortunate we've got each other." Vivienne touched Jesse's shoulder.

Florence clutched her hands at her waist. "Since we've been sharing, I have something to tell you all."

A chipmunk rustled through the nearby leaves and dashed up a tree.

Jesse cocked his head at Florence. "What is it?"

"I've secured a good position for myself, and I plan to leave for Detroit within the week."

"What?" Jesse gaped at her.

Vivienne hugged her sister. "That's so exciting."

"Where? What are you doing?" Jesse rubbed his forehead.

"Many years ago, Father brought me to a railroad investors' meeting in New York."

"I remember."

"I met a lady there who said if I ever wished to learn more about business to contact her." She shrugged.

"I thought the men actually shut you out of the meeting and you only spoke to the cleaning lady." Frankly, he'd thought Florence had made the whole thing up.

Flo grinned. "Yes. Except she was no ordinary cleaning lady. She's a wealthy businesswoman. And my new boss."

He arched an eyebrow. He couldn't have her living in Detroit without protection. "You'll live where?"

"In one of her homes. She's currently residing elsewhere but she has several servants who will be there to help." As the breeze kicked up again, Florence clutched her hat. "And I'll work diligently to procure you a placement in her business, Jesse. Have no worries."

He heard Maggie's almost inaudible gasp and resisted the urge to reach and squeeze her hand. When he turned to look at her, he caught her stricken look.

He had the feeling Maggie wasn't concerned about Flo leaving, but rather the possibility that he might. And that trilled something in his masculine pride that he'd never before sensed—a connection of possible permanence.

His face heated. What did he have to offer? A pittance of a schoolteacher's wages.

Maggie deserved better.

Chapter Eight

The steep steps of the Indian Dormitory building, which housed the Mackinac Public School, loomed imposing before Jesse. *First day of school.* He'd never stepped inside a public education building in his life.

"Good morning, Mr. Huntington." Miss Dearing moved alongside him. The attractive blonde, with a willowy figure, taught the younger students.

"Good day." Would it be?

She laughed. "You look petrified."

He rubbed his chin. "Maybe merely terrified."

"Ah." She smiled and gestured toward the stairway. "I've sometimes wondered if these stairs were built on a steep incline to impress the Indian families whose children were brought here."

"Or to deter the parents from running in to take their children back home." Jesse blinked back a memory of facing similar steps, albeit brick not wood, at the boarding school he'd attended in Richmond, Virginia. Maybe what he was feeling right now wasn't concern over his lack of public-school experience but the unease he'd felt every year when Father had unceremoniously deposited him on the school steps. At least Rutherford Huntington had escorted his son there, unlike many parents at that dismal school.

"Why would they want to prevent their children from receiving a proper education?" She held her skirts aside with her left hand and clutched the rail with her right hand as she began to climb the stairs.

"I don't know much about the values of the local natives."

Miss Dearing cast him a sideways glance. "You'll find that we have many Indian students among our classes. And Métis children as well."

"Truly?" He followed her up the stairs and caught up to her, stepping alongside her.

"It would behoove you to learn more of their culture." She definitely sounded like a frosty schoolmarm.

"Agreed." He offered what he hoped was a charming smile.

They reached the landing at the top. "If you need help, please feel free to call on me after school." She placed her hand gently on his.

When he looked into her eyes, a soft lavender, he didn't see the spark that always loomed in Maggie's. He searched her gaze for a moment, not wanting to see any attraction there. Such a situation could be disastrous for him as a first-year teacher.

Nothing there but a sweet, clear, kind look. "Thank you, Miss Dearing."

She released his hand and drew in a deep breath. She turned toward the street. Jesse followed her gaze. A breeze threatened to lift his hat, and he grabbed it. Despite the thick ribbon that secured her bonnet, his fellow teacher grasped her hat brim.

"Who is that young man down at the street, Mr. Huntington?"

At first Jesse didn't see anyone walking. Then he spied the dray which moved at no more than a snail's crawl by the school. *Maggie.* Even from this distance, he could spy her red cheeks. Had she seen the two of them talking?

He cleared his throat. "Oh, that's Mickey. He drives for Mr. Stan Danner and also drives for my family at night."

"How strange that he'd lurk there." Her lips twitched downward.

"Perhaps he's come to bid me a good start to the school year. We've become friends." Why then, did he wish it was more? But when Jesse waved at Maggie, she didn't wave back.

Miss Dearing quirked a dark eyebrow at him. "Perhaps the superintendent tipped him to ensure you'd actually showed up."

"What?"

She grinned. "There's a betting pool going on down at Foster's Tavern as to how long you'll last."

"Is that so?"

"Yes. One fellow bet you'd not show up at all. And the longest bet is that you'll be gone by Christmas."

By Christmas? Wasn't that what his sister Florence had implied, when she'd departed the previous week? That she'd find him a spot by then for all of them to come to Detroit. He'd never thought he'd have to rely upon his sister to help him find work as a businessman. But if he did, then he'd be leaving behind. . . His gaze fixed on the best friend he'd ever had—as well as the prettiest.

With a flick of the reins, Maggie sent her team forward.

First day of school and the pretty schoolteacher was already putting the moves on Jesse. Steam boiled up inside of Maggie as she directed Moo and Bear around a corner and over to Eli's house. He'd not shown up this morning and Mr. Danner had asked her to check on her dray partner. He'd given her a route to do if Eli accompanied her and an alternate plan if he was unable to work.

They soon pulled down the carriage house drive to the mint green home of Eli and his bride. The door at the exterior stairway flew open and Abigail emerged.

"I thought I saw you, Mickey." Wrapped in a too-large robe, Abigail looked even younger than her twenty years. More like a girl.

"Where's your husband? Sleepin' off your good cooking?" Maggie tried to ask the other woman questions like her brothers might have done.

"He's sick."

Maggie's first inclination was to gush over how sorry she was. But her brothers wouldn't have. "Sorry to hear that. Tell him to get on the mend soon."

"Pray for him, Mickey."

Maggie touched her hat brim, like Russell would have, but didn't reply. Of course she'd pray for him, but a man wouldn't necessarily shout that back. This was getting harder and harder to play this role. Bits of herself were being chipped away every time she acted this part. She directed the horses around and back to the street. Since she didn't have Eli, she'd need to run up to the fort. Which meant she had to drive past the school again.

Why did she have these strong feelings for Jesse? She'd been courted before, not that Jesse Huntington was courting her, but never had her heart's yearnings overcome her like they did when she was with him. But there would never be a romantic relationship between them. At least not one that would lead to what she really desired—husband, home, children, and a future together. They had become fast friends. But that was as far as things would go. One day his future and finances would alter dramatically, and he'd be back in the good graces of high society. Wealthy people always seemed to pull out of these things in the end. Florence's departure illustrated that truth. Maggie chewed her lip.

She directed the horses to the wharf and retrieved their cargo destined for the fort. Then she continued on her route. Every time she went to Fort Mackinac alone, she was on pins and needles. Sergeant Mauvais always seemed to show up wherever she was, which was usually at the Quartermaster's. And even though he had no business there, the man snooped about as the soldiers unloaded all the boxes. Thankfully, Dora had never crossed Maggie's path again. But maybe the sergeant had ensured that the beautiful officer's daughter didn't have an opportunity to converse with the lowly dray driver.

They approached the fort. The greens were empty save for the private at the gate, a handsome tall blond of about twenty. "*Ole nopea, on pian juhla.*"

Maggie frowned at him. "Speak English." She recognized one of the Finnish words as "hurry" – she'd heard a lot of Finnish lumberjacks around Pickford but hadn't picked up much of the language.

"Sorry." The man lifted a hand in apology. "You need hurry with these things—there is party."

"The horses only go so fast, soldier." Maggie spit in the dirt.

"Go then!" He waved forward. "You get trouble with sergeant if his lady doesn't get her t'ings."

Shoulders stiffening, Maggie flicked the reins.

When she pulled in behind the Quartermaster's building, Sergeant Mauvais ran toward her, his face mottled red. "Where've you been?"

When it looked like he might try to climb up beside her, Maggie instinctively grabbed the whip, as Pa had taught her, and which Danner had sanctioned in such instances. "Get back!"

"Dora Witherell has returned this morning and the comestibles we ordered aren't here."

Don't think like a woman, think like a man. Maggie's hands shook, so she pressed them down on her thighs. "First of all, Mister—"

"That's sergeant—"

Maggie waved her hand dismissively. "First of all, sergeant." She leaned forward, whip still in hand. "I'm not responsible for your orders coming or not. That's whoever you're doing business with."

He scowled. "Still you could have gotten this up here quicker."

Maggie couldn't have the sergeant thinking he could bully her. "You're lucky you even got these supplies today."

He narrowed his eyes at her. "Why is that?"

"Boss didn't mention any rush nor did the dockmaster."

Mauvais fisted his hands. "They were told."

"Mr. Danner would've said."

"Well, that. . ." he burst into a string of profanities so foul that Maggie fought the urge to wince, "...dockmaster was told."

Although she was quaking inside, Maggie shrugged. "Dockmaster has plenty other concerns."

"Now you see here." Spittle flung out with each word he slung. "We might be leaving this. . ." more profanity ensued, "island soon, when the state takes over, but the army must remain a priority."

She couldn't help herself. "This here's a mighty small army outpost that's closing soon. You're concerned about a spoiled girl's party, not the military's needs."

The man's lips drew together so tightly that they almost disappeared. He stared at her for the longest time and Maggie met his furious gaze. He took two steps closer to the dray and peered up at her, his features beginning to soften.

Oh no, she'd overplayed her hand. He was looking at her too intently and the steam had gone out of him. Did he know?

What have I done?

Chapter Nine

"Can I put up the October calendar?" Opal Duvall stood in front of Jesse's desk and rocked back and forth.

"May I?" He hoped his gentle reminder wouldn't frighten the skittish child.

Her lips formed an "O". "You want to do it, Mr. Huntington?"

He chuckled. "No, but since *you* are asking permission, you're asking if you *may* change the calendar." The previous afternoon, the children had made their own classroom calendar during art time.

"It's too heavy for her." Benjy, a tall Chippewa boy, whose given name was Bemidii, waved his hand over the heavy canvas calendar.

Tristan, who possessed the most serious expression Jesse had ever seen on a child, unfolded his lanky fourteen-year-old frame from his too-small desk. "I'm the oldest student. I should put it up."

Tears gathered in Opal's light eyes. "I can stand on a chair."

As classroom chatter increased, Jesse raised his hand. "That's enough." Thankfully his class stopped talking. A month earlier he'd have had to whack his ruler on the desk to silence them. Surprisingly, when they'd learned that he'd never bring a ruler down on any of their hands much less a rod on their backs, the students had become more compliant. The carrot motivated them much better than the stick.

"The calendar needs to be where all the pupils can reach it because we plan to continue decorating it." He picked up a felt cut-out of a dray and another of a hammer and displayed them. "If we achieve all our math and English goals this week, then Mr. Christy, the Master Craftsman at the Grand Hotel, will bring us over for a visit and demonstrate some basic woodworking skills."

Bea raised her hand. "Can I sit up *front* with the dray driver on our way to the Grand?"

"First of all—it is *may* I, not can I. I already know you *can* or are able to do so. Use of the word *may* is asking permission." He arched an eyebrow at her.

"May I?"

"No, Miss Duvall, you will have the very important job of watching over our youngest students." He intended to ride next to Maggie and enjoy himself. None of his students would be any the wiser that he was sitting next to a young woman who'd become very dear to him. As far as they knew, "Mickey" was their male driver.

The girl sighed.

Jesse continued, "In return for your assistance you'll be able to sit with Mickey on the drive back."

Bea whooped. Jack rolled his eyes.

Jesse cleared his throat. "I expect you'll not display such behaviors inside the Grand Hotel."

Bea nodded primly.

Waving wildly, Jack Welling looked like he might burst. "What about the Harvest Festival?"

Jesse pressed his eyes closed for a moment. He simply couldn't reprimand the boy, whose mother was terribly ill. He nodded and met Jack's gaze. "If all of you are well-behaved, then the Grand will host us at the close of their season for the festival."

The entire classroom erupted in pandemonium until Jesse waved his arms overhead. "I only told you what the Grand Hotel required. Let me explain what I'm expecting in order for us to have our Harvest Festival during school time."

He reviewed their agenda, detailing expectations of each grade level. Then he gestured to Opal and to Tristan. "Our eldest student shall assist our youngest in affixing the calendar to the wall." He pointed to the spot where he'd hammered in two nails earlier that morning. Soon the two had the cloth calendar hanging from its top loops, which they'd wrapped around the nails.

Looking out at his very own class of students, warmth flowed through Jesse. Pleasure at forging relationships, at accomplishing the task of settling uprooted children into a safe and secure environment, and at teaching them skills that could last a lifetime all combined to bring him a joy he'd never known.

Or maybe it was because every night he returned home to Maggie.

"I can't believe Festival Day is already here." Maggie leaned her head against Moo's neck and stroked his side. "I feel guilty that I'm glad Miss Dearing's class won't be coming, too." The younger class had too many children sick. *Poor kiddies.*

The brown and white Percheron nickered.

"I'll pray for the sick students, their parents, and that none of the staff takes ill, either." She patted Moo's neck.

"You're a good girl, aren't you?" Maggie headed to the other side of the dray. "Bear, I think you're ready to go home to Pickford, aren't you?"

Strong winds in the straits had prevented the pair from being transported back to the mainland the previous week. "I'm relieved you and Moo got to stay here with me a while longer, too." She stroked Bear's black neck. "You're such a handsome and good boy. What would I do without you here?"

"Ahem." Mr. Danner came alongside her. "You ready to head down to the school?"

"Eli's getting the last few bales of hay for the kids to sit on." He'd not be coming with her, though.

"He's becoming a fine driver under your tutelage."

"Thank you."

"And I imagine you've heard. . ."

She nodded. "A baby is on the way." Abigail had told Vivienne who in turn had told her family and Jesse. So Maggie had known even before Eli had shyly shared his happy news with her. Would Maggie, too, one day become a mother? And why did her imaginings include little babies with dark hair like Jesse's?

"There's Eli now. He has another surprise for you later."

"What?"

Mr. Danner grinned enigmatically but didn't respond. He pointed to the driver's seat. "Hop on up and get those children up to the Grand. I've heard they've been barely able to contain themselves all week."

"Yes, sir." She offered a mock salute.

Soon she headed out with Moo and Bear toward the school.

Brisk air swirled falling maple leaves around the wagon wheels as she drove. A street sweeper waved to her as she passed, and she nodded. Ahead, two older women stepped

101

into the road, and Maggie eased her Percherons to a halt. She didn't need the hay all tumbling off the dray bed. Hopefully the rest of the way she'd have no bicyclists darting in front of her. Unlikely to happen since the tourists had now returned home except for a stray few. She'd learned to not worry herself about islanders on bicycles, for most handled themselves expertly around the carriages and drays.

Within a few minutes, she pulled up by the school. Jesse, dressed in cream-colored dress pants, a navy vest, and a striped navy and cream jacket looked the epitome of elegance. He wore a bowler hat today and carried a large box.

Jack Welling, a frequent visitor at the Huntingtons' home, led the group of students down to the dray. "Girls first." Although he waved to the back of the dray and smiled, when Jack turned his pixyish face toward her she caught him wrinkling his nose. He mouthed, 'Should be boys first' at her and she couldn't quell a laugh that escaped.

Once the girls had settled, the boys jumped in, making enough noise to wake the occupants of the St. Anne's graveyard on the hill far away. Maggie put her fingers between her teeth and whistled.

It actually worked. They quieted down. She smirked in satisfaction. How did Jesse manage these imps every day? Although the idea of having her own children seemed a good one, she couldn't fathom trying to teach someone else's offspring. Unless they were learning about horses—that she could manage.

Jesse got up and slid next to her on the bench. "Good day, Mickey. Or should I say, good morning Loser?"

She jabbed her elbow into his side. "If you hadn't cheated, I'd have won that last round of Rummy." More likely he'd won because she'd been too busy gazing across the table at him. At least Vivienne didn't catch Maggie making eyes at her brother, like she had the previous game.

He raised his palms and splayed his fingers. "I never cheat."

"Ha!" She looked back. "All set, Jack?"

He gave her a thumb's up. She turned back around.

Jesse leaned toward her. "Mrs. Welling is not improving, I fear."

"The ladies at the steam laundry said Mrs. Duvall is also very ill. Bed-bound I heard."

Jesse frowned. "Bea hasn't said anything. But Opal has been very quiet the past few days."

"Keep praying for all of them." She looked at him as she forced back tears. "You do pray for your students, don't you?"

"I didn't used to pray much at all."

"No?"

"But something about this island. Something about being here. . ." His voice trailed off. Although she was looking ahead, she caught him staring at her out of the corner of her eye.

Jesse cleared his throat. "I find myself getting reacquainted with God after a long time of silence."

What did she say to that? "That's good." That was all she could manage?

"Say, would you help me rehearse my lines for Vivienne's play?"

"Sure." Vivienne was putting on a little production of children searching for, and finding, a treasure and being grateful for their good fortune. That was part of the Harvest Festival later in the afternoon.

As they rolled along toward the hotel, the children sang "The Farmer in the Dell" in the back while Jesse murmured his lines.

"Jesse, you're so good with your varying voices for the different characters."

"I better be." He laughed. "Vivienne will scold me if I don't perform the way she wishes."

"Yup. Vivie is a demanding taskmaster." Maggie shook her head. "That's why I don't volunteer to do anything but drive for her."

"Because you're perfect at that?"

"Well, if you say so." She grinned.

"Vivienne says so, as does Mr. Danner."

What a shame that although she was an expert at dealing with horses, society wouldn't acknowledge that. And the only way she'd be able to run a farm would be in secret, as she might be able to do one day, for her father. One day though. . .

As they rounded the tight corner, Jesse's shoulder and thigh pressed in against her, stirring an awareness of his masculine presence that she didn't need showing on her face. She didn't mind, but if anyone saw her rosy cheeks. . . He pulled away, grabbing the side of the bench.

"Sorry."

They drew up front, instead of behind, the beautiful white Grand Hotel building that dominated the cliffside. With the largest porch in the world, the huge painted pine structure commanded the attention of anyone who'd visited the island. Normally Maggie would bring the dray to the back, for unloading by employees. But today they were met in front, under the high arches, by Mr. Christy, who had helped set up all manner of Harvest Festival activities for the children. His wife, who owned the tea shop and bakery, was supplying cider and doughnuts and cookies.

Once the children, and Jesse, had exited the dray, a bicyclist moved alongside Maggie on the driver's side. She looked down into Eli's beaming face. "What are you doing here, Eli?"

"Mr. Danner said you get to attend. You can stay here."

She frowned in disbelief. "Why didn't he say so to me?"

"That's his surprise for you." Eli moved his bike to the rack on the side.

I get to participate and remain. What a day this could be. Jesse turned and looked at her, his handsome face wearing a quizzical expression.

Eli hopped up. "Danner said it's high time I did the dray run on my own and it's also time for you to get an extra day off."

"Really?" She'd loved their autumn fairs in Pickford. They'd always been so fun.

"Get down, *man*, and I'll be on my way." Eli beamed up at her.

Now, an hour later, Maggie threw her third-in-a-row ringer of horseshoes around the pole. Every one of her tosses had hit perfectly.

Beside her, Jesse groaned. "That's embarrassing."

Jack handed Maggie a sugar-dusted doughnut. "Congratulations, Mickey." He turned to face Jesse. "Ain't nothin' embarrassing about having a drayman beat you, Jesse."

Jesse cleared his throat.

"Mr. Huntington, that is." Jack made a face. "It ain't like some dumb old girl beat you, like Bea beat me in the potato sack race."

Maggie stifled a laugh.

Opal ran toward them, crying, crimson streaking her hands. "I got cut!" Her heart-rending shriek made Maggie want to cover her ears, she was so loud, but Jesse bent and wrapped an arm around the girl.

"Let me see." He pulled out his creamy linen handkerchief and wiped at her palms.

Bea ran toward them, face contorting in disgust. "She's only got a bit of raspberry jam on her hands, that's all."

"I got cut." Opal glared up at her sister.

But when Jesse kept wiping, the child's hands showed nothing but a thin bloodless scratch. He held the handkerchief out to Maggie. "Smells like raspberry to me, Mickey. What do you think?"

Maggie bent and sniffed the fruity scent. "You have raspberry jam for blood! You're one lucky girl, Opal." She patted the girl on the head. "No wonder you seem so sweet." She winked at the child.

Bea rolled her eyes. "You're only encouraging her, Mr. Hadley."

Maggie shrugged and pulled a coin out of her pocket and handed it to the younger girl. "Go buy a trinket at that booth over yonder, for your Ma. Somethin' to cheer her up."

Opal blinked up at her through wet eyes. "Thank you, sir." She skipped off, clutching the coin in her fist. Bea followed slowly behind.

"Nice of you." Jesse inclined his head so close to her that she could feel his warm breath on her wind-chilled cheeks.

Heartbeat ratcheting upward, Maggie stayed stock still. If they were alone, if he leaned in closer, she could bend toward him and kiss him.

But they weren't alone.

Yet how she longed for that possibility. And for more time together.

October's nip had necessitated Jesse moving Maggie from the carriage house into the Huntingtons' larger home and into an upstairs bedroom, but with November fast approaching Jesse had to ensure they'd all be warm. To that effect he'd asked Mr. Christy to help them obtain more wood to burn. Jesse rode one of the Wellings' bicycles back from work, expecting to meet the man at the house. Maggie was supposed to have driven the loaded dray up to the bluffs. But as he arrived, he saw that the dray parked in their drive stood empty. Perhaps Mr. Christy had helpers who unloaded the wood with him. One could hope.

He strode up the drive, which could use more crushed stone added, and to the brick walkway. Light snow dusted the holly bushes edging the house. Laughter carried from inside as he opened the door.

"I'm home, Mother." He removed his hat and scarf and hung them on the hall tree and then did the same with his wool coat.

"We're in the parlor," Vivienne called out.

Jesse entered the room, which would soon be blessedly warmer after the supply of wood.

Garrett Christy nodded at Jesse as he accepted a cup of tea from Mother. "Thank you ma'am. And good to see you again, Jesse."

"Thank you for bringing the wood to us."

Christy's teacup clinked as he set it down hard in its china saucer. "I was only making a social call today, Mr. Huntington."

Mother blinked up at him, that strange absent gleam still in her eyes that had been there since Father's death. "Son, Mr. Christy says he needs to speak with you privately."

Jesse's gut clenched. *No wood. A private matter.* This could not be good. He'd paid the man before he'd departed for the mainland. It couldn't be money. Or had the price risen?

Mother rose and then brushed at her skirts to straighten them. "I'll leave you gentlemen to your business." She offered Jesse a charming Southern belle half-smile before bestowing the same upon Garrett Christy, and then departed the room.

"Best sit down." Garrett's dark eyebrows drew together. "I have a few questions for you."

"All right." Jesse lowered to the divan and poured himself some tea, his hands shaking enough to rattle the teapot's lid.

"When me and my wife first moved here, Mrs. Welling educated me on the construction of many of these homes up on the bluff. She grew up here."

"Sir?"

"Most of these newer homes on the bluff, like this one, were built for summer-only living. And with the hard winter we may get, you may not be able to keep this house warm even if you fill the fireplaces ten times a day."

"What?" But somewhere in the back of his memory, Jesse recalled his father saying something to that effect. It had never concerned him before. Now it did. He dragged his fingers through the side of his hair.

"I didn't want to discuss this problem with your mother as she seems rather. . ." Christy rubbed his dark beard.

"My mother hasn't recovered from the many losses she's suffered."

"I understand. All that loss can make a person feel like goin' away to their own little world. My wife got like that for a while after her um. . . ordeal."

Mrs. Rebecca Christy had nearly been killed by a deranged man when she was younger. She'd been an encouragement to the Huntingtons during the worst of Mother's spells, sending up notes and treats.

"I appreciate you not asking Mother." What was he to do? The tepid tea only exacerbated his chill. "You didn't bring us back any wood, then?"

"I did. It's down at the docks. But Mrs. Welling was right—only a few homes up here can be occupied year 'round."

"I can't afford to rent someone else's home." Where would they go? Jesse covered his eyes with his hands and rubbed his face briskly against the headache that was building there.

"The way I see it you got a few choices." Christy arched a brow. "You can try to suffer through the winter, maybe move your family down to the first floor. We can ask some of the old timers on the island for advice. We can look for rentals for you."

"I couldn't pay."

Christy raised his broad hands. "I don't rightly know what we'll find, but we won't know unless we ask around. Maybe someone's got a winter-worthy warm house they'll let you use if you'll maintain it. Keep up the place while they're gone during the off-season."

Pride leapt up and grabbed Jesse by the throat. He couldn't manage a word. His family wouldn't take charity. But how long would it be before all the windows in the house iced over?

The craftsman rose. "I'll check on things for you. And Maggie and I will bring some wood up tomorrow after school."

Jesse nodded and stood. Mr. Christy had figured out early on that Maggie was not a young man and he'd not betrayed her confidence. This was a good man. Someone they could all trust.

"I'll let myself out, no need." The broad-shouldered man, who was still wearing his Mackinaw coat, headed out.

Stay and freeze? Or swallow his pride if a warm home was offered?

His sister entered the parlor, holding a small tray of cookies. "Goodness, I know his wife is an amazing baker, like his sister, but my treats shouldn't have caused Mr. Christy to run off."

She set the tray down then turned to warm her hands by the fire. "When does that next load of wood get delivered? I feel like I am parsing them out like in that *Little Match Girl* story."

Jesse laughed. "Things are not quite that extreme."

"My lips are turning blue."

"Not quite."

"It feels like it when the wind rattles the windows and seeps in the cracks."

"I thought you and Mother were going to add some more of those heavy draperies you found in the closet."

"We did, but there were only enough for the bedrooms."

He could convert the parlor to a sleeping room and the office as well. But where would they all fit?

Lord grant me wisdom. Give us provision.

Chapter Ten

November already. Maggie sat at the Huntingtons' kitchen table, the scent of rising dough and cinnamon wafting from the covered bowls she'd set nearby. She'd received starter dough from Mrs. Christy earlier that day. Now her own loaves would be ready that evening. She washed up and sat down to copy Mrs. Christy's recipe onto a card for her own files.

Jesse sat at his small desk in the adjacent parlor, grading papers. He looked up and smiled at her and winked.

She blushed and returned her focus to the bread's ingredients.

Mrs. Huntington carried the silver mail salver to the table. "I'm afraid the butler didn't bring this to you earlier, my dear."

Maggie searched the woman's placid face, to see if she was jesting. She looked serious. There was no butler nor any other type of servant in the household. "Thank you, ma'am."

"You're welcome." She swiveled and silently exited the room.

Jesse's sad eyes followed his mother.

Maggie turned the envelope over and her heart leapt when she recognized Pa's scrawl. Chicken-scratching was what Ma called it. Maggie chewed on her lower lip. Pa never wrote letters unless he wanted a point to be made or if some bad news had to be conveyed. Ma handled all the letter writing even to his kin, with Pa giving ideas of what to tell folks. Would Pa be telling her to come back home? He said he'd write if her brothers got work or if things changed for the better on the farm.

She unsealed the envelope and retrieved the letter.

Dear Margaret,

I have news. Some good some bad. No fears – God is good. First, your Ma has been real sick. But our neighbor, Mrs. Crist, has been tending to her as have I. Ma's on the mend now.

Maggie exhaled a breath. Several women Ma's age on the island had died recently from a vicious illness.

John got work in Newberry building that new asylum. Russell is fully recovered. And here's the best news of all, my girl – you can come home soon. Russ wants his job back with Mr. Danner and he wants to get over to the island before the hard freeze so that you can catch a boat back home before then.

So we'll be able to have a family Christmas together. I know how you love all the celebrations. And Ma would be cheered by your return home.

Home? Why did her heart sink at the thought? She ought to be excited. *Thrilled, even.* The place where she loved to be and was fully loved and known. But as she glanced across the dining room to Jesse in the parlor, she had to face the truth. She was in love. In love with a schoolteacher with a one-year contract who could be gone at any time. A gentleman from a social status so far above her level that she couldn't even fathom it. Whether Jesse would admit it or not, at some point his family's connections would have to result

112

in more lucrative employment. A business position far from here. Far from her.

She dropped the letter into her lap, running her fingers over the smooth paper.

One day soon she'd have to return home. How many days from now until her brother would arrive? She'd pack her bag, wave goodbye to Jesse, hug his sister and mother, and then head back to Pickford. She'd return to the same home, same family—but her heart would be heavier from that day on.

A tear escaped down her cheek, and she swiped at it.

"What's wrong?" Jesse's eyes flashed concern.

She shook her head. "My mother's been ill."

He rose and came to her side. "Will she be all right?" He gently touched her shoulder.

Maggie nodded as her tears overflowed, not because of her mother who she was sure would recover, but because she'd be leaving him. "Yes, she'll be fine."

"I'm glad." He wrapped an arm around her shoulder and squeezed.

She's seen him perform this affectionate gesture a hundred times with his sisters and mother but when Maggie looked up at him, she saw something more than the concern that would normally be there. In his eyes was a longing that she recognized, one simmering in her own heart. His eyes widened and he brushed the hair back from her forehead and then leaned toward her. Her heartbeat hitched in her chest.

Footsteps sounded in the parlor and Jesse released her. Both turned to see Vivienne toting a large box into the room.

"Mind if I join you? I've got to get these theater props finished."

Guilt must have shown on their faces because Vivienne glanced back and forth between them a few times.

Jesse gestured toward the letter. "Maggie's mom has been very sick but she's on the mend now."

113

"Oh. Good." Vivienne set the crate of fabrics on the table. She removed lace and ribbon spools and then pushed them around the table like she did when she was nervous. "I wish I had a complete room dedicated to my creations."

Maggie looked up. "I think you'll have more space soon for your projects."

The girl's fair eyebrows drew together. "Why is that?"

Trying to keep her tone even, Maggie squared her shoulders, feeling the cotton fabric of her work shirt bunch between her shoulder blades. "My Pa says my brother Russell will be coming soon to take his position back. So I'll need to leave."

"Leave?" Jesse seemed to suck in a breath. His handsome features tugged in concern. Did he care as much as she did?

He must.

Yet even with this bad news, the thought that Jesse Huntington, who had one year earlier been the son of one of the wealthiest men in America, cared for her, buoyed her spirits.

"I'm afraid so."

"When?"

"By Christmas."

"Is Russell returning?" Vivienne's voice emerged almost shyly.

Maggie cocked her head at the younger woman, who was chewing her lip.

Vivienne moved closer to her brother. "Didn't Flo say she'll know by Christmas if they can offer you a position in Detroit?"

"Oh." Maggie stiffened. Why hadn't he said anything?

Jesse's cheeks turned a warm shade of red as he patted his coat pocket. "We've been passing around her latest letter. Would you like to see it?"

No, I wouldn't. "Certainly."

He handed the missive to her and Maggie forced herself to touch the warm paper that had been tucked so close to Jesse's heart. Where she wanted to be. But that would not be happening now. Nor had it ever been a possibility.

She scanned Florence's letter. Clearly she was excited about her job. And she had a position possibility for Jesse that would suit him. Florence was happy. Maggie gave the letter back to Jesse.

"Before you leave us, Miss Hadley, I'd like to share some business advice with you to pass on to your father."

Miss Hadley? Now she was Miss Hadley, again?

"Certainly, I'm sure he'd appreciate it, as would I." Not as much as she'd have appreciated other things, though.

"Good, then we'll begin as soon as you're finished penning your response to your family and I am done grading my papers."

"What specific advice do you have?"

"Some suggestions about collecting debt and about putting some teeth in his contracts."

She stifled a bitter laugh. How ironic coming from someone who had delayed repaying her hard-working father until the last moment possible. She'd been a fool.

Jesse would be going on his way. So would Maggie.

She rose from the table. "I'm going up to stoke my fireplace before I go to bed." Even doing so would barely take the chill from the room, and certainly not from her heart.

Jesse surveyed his classroom, satisfaction surging through him more rampantly than in any of his previous endeavors. "Class, since it's the month of Thanksgiving, I'd like you to write down three things you're thankful for this year. Then fold that slip of paper up and bring it to the front for our cornucopia." He patted the wicker basket that Mrs. Christy had sent in early that month, crammed full of cookies for the children.

Soon Opal Duvall joined him at his desk. She handed her folded paper to him, then slipped her tiny hand into Jesse's. "You're the bestest teacher ever, Mr. Huntington."

"Best." Jesse adjusted his tie.

"That's not humble to agree with her." Ephraim scowled at Jesse from his seat in the front row.

"I'm not agreeing with Opal, I'm correcting her." Though he ought not do so, given everything the poor child was going through at home. Still, this was his job.

"You shouldn't look a gift horse in the mouth, my Ma says." Bea crossed her arms over her chest.

Jesse frowned and was about to explain that the expression didn't apply to the situation, but Jack elbowed forward.

"Yeah!" Obviously Jack didn't understand the gift horse analogy either.

He bit back a retort.

Jesse squeezed the little girl's hand. "First of all, Opal, instead of bestest you should have said, 'best—as in best teacher ever'—when you spoke."

Jack opened his mouth to protest and Jesse pointed at him. "Not one word until I have finished."

The boy tucked his chin against his flannel-covered chest.

"Next, I did not agree with Opal, Ephraim, as far as my capabilities." He met the child's gaze. "In fact, in all humility I can say I am a true novice at teaching." He did love the children far more than his novice's heart would admit.

"What's a novice?" Jack, despite his proclivity for *improper* grammar, did enjoy increasing his vocabulary.

"Oh, I know!" Mary Elizabeth, seated adjacent Ephraim, waved her hand. "It's in the Catholic church when. . ."

Jesse shook his head. "No, you mean *novitiate* that's not the same as novice."

"Oh." A tear spilled onto her cheek.

"It's all right, Mary Elizabeth, that was an excellent attempt."

Bea brought her folded paper to the front and smirked. "She was wrong."

Jesse fixed the older girl with what he hoped was a piercing gaze. But when she rolled her eyes and walked away, he figured he must have failed.

Opal patted his arm. "You are my favorite teacher. Does that make you the best?"

"No, not really." Jesse pointed out the window to where snow was gently filtering down. "I could choose a favorite child in the upcoming January snowman contest but that would not make their rendering of a frozen man to be of an excellent quality."

"Do you have a favorite student?" Opal's hopeful gaze stung his heart.

He leaned in. "I have favorites." He winked at her.

"Who are they?" Ephraim lifted one dark eyebrow.

"Do you really want to know?" He stood.

"Yes."

"All right students, stand in a line here." He gestured to the left side of the blackboard.

His pupils rose from their desks, with a commotion, and formed a queue. When they'd all settled down, he pointed to Marcus, who stood in the front. "Write Ben's full name down on the board please, then take your seat."

"Middle name, too?"

"No."

Marcus scowled but then wrote out Benjamin's first and last name. He stomped off to his seat. Jesse gestured for Opal to move forward. "Write Mary Elizabeth's name on the board."

"But she's not up here in line."

"She will be in a moment." Jesse caught the older girl's gaze and quirked his index finger at her, to come forward. "And please help Opal with the spelling."

They continued on until the last child, Benjamin, grinned at Jesse. "I reckon you want me to write Ephraim's name up here, don't ya?"

"You're a smart boy, Benjamin."

The children all returned to their desks, smiling.

Opal raised her hand and glanced around at her classmates. "So, we're all your favorites?"

He pointed to the board. "That's my list, so yes, you're all my favorites."

Was it his imagination or did the children in his classroom have their chins all lifted a smidge higher now?

He grinned, sure that they did.

"Now, class, next we're going to expand on our writing task for the day. So I want you to write one paragraph on something you hope to be grateful for in the upcoming year."

Would 1895 be a good year for him if it didn't include Maggie?

Chapter Eleven

The white limestone walls of Fort Mackinac gleamed in the sun on the hillside, taunting Maggie as December's frigid breezes gusted in off the Straits. Maggie directed her Percherons to pull the fully loaded dray away from the docks. Maggie puffed out breaths above the heavy blue scarf that Rebecca Christy had knit for her as an early Christmas gift. She tugged on the matching knit cap. With both items on, she'd almost startled herself earlier when she'd looked into a mirror and could have been glimpsing a reflection of her eldest brother, whose eye color and slightly almond shape matched hers perfectly.

She'd directed the team onto the snow-covered streets as soft clumpy flakes of snow whirled down. The world was quieter with the filmy white cover. Smoke rose upward from occupied homes' chimneys—easy to tell which houses were empty for the off-season.

Moo and Bear navigated the turns and soon, headed up the steep incline to the back of the fort. Which soldiers would off-load their supplies and bring them in? With the fort closing soon, she prayed Sergeant Mauvais would be gone, but Eli had said the man had been thrown out of Foster's Saloon the previous weekend for disorderly behavior.

Eli and Mr. Danner had earlier in the day brought the Mackinac Island students up for an early Christmas party at the Commander's Residence. It would have been nice to have Jesse there as she arrived. But that wasn't to be. She chewed on her lower lip as she approached the gate.

A lone soldier huddled inside the wooden guard shack. Private Abernathy stepped out and waved to her. "Good morning, Hadley."

"What are you doin' out here, Abernathy?"

The clerk wiped at his beet-red nose. "We're short-staffed with all the departures."

The fort would soon be closed. "Was Mauvais one of those?" A girl could hope. And pray.

Abernathy grunted. "You'd think so, after that episode in town, but no, he's still here."

Her heart sank. So not only was the horrible man still there but also Miss Dearing presided over the Commander's party where the beautiful teacher could demonstrate how she was so much more suitable for Jesse than Maggie would ever be.

I shouldn't be so uncharitable.

Miss Dearing had never been anything but kind to Maggie in their few exchanges. And Jesse had never reported that the teacher had ever done anything to suggest she was setting her cap for him. Still, with Maggie about to depart for the mainland, she couldn't help her wild imaginings.

A gust of wind penetrated her heavy wool coat and swirled snow up around the private's legs. Moo and Bear shifted in their braces.

"It's an ill wind that brings no good." Abernathy laughed at his own pronouncement of the saying. "I'm off to Lieutenant Geary's home in a moment to grab some hot cider. Stop back by here on your way out and I'll bring you a mug, too."

"They're holding the party there?"

"Yes, special announcement coming, I heard."

120

"Oh?"

"Yes, I believe the captain's daughter will finally receive a ring from the lieutenant."

"Which won't make Mauvais any too happy." Maybe that's why he'd gotten into trouble at the saloon.

"Yeah, you can bet he's not invited to that party." Abernathy laughed.

Maggie flicked the reins and they rolled on into the fort.

As she neared the Quartermaster's building, a burly man with sergeant's stripes, the only man in the lightly occupied fort to possess such a rank, swiveled toward her. She cringed. *Mauvais.*

She unconsciously jerked the horses to a halt, startling herself when they stopped. The man scowled at her but was that also a leer beneath his whiskers as he waved to move behind the Quartermaster's building instead of into the courtyard.

She hesitated.

He bellowed, "Forward!" resting his hand on his hip.

Swallowing hard, she directed Moo and Bear into position.

One of the privates strode into the space between the Quartermaster's building and the adjacent one. Before he turned his back to her, he gave her a wicked grin.

Fear prickled her skin.

"It's *Miss* Hadley, isn't it?"

When Sergeant Mauvais jumped onto the back of the dray and began laughing, Maggie looked for her escape.

But where could she run?

The occupant of the beautiful two-story officer's quarters, Lieutenant Woodbridge Geary, offered the children a tour of the rooms, all of which had been decorated beautifully for Christmas. Not like the Huntington's place on the Charleston Battery, but beautiful, nonetheless. Holly berries and leaves were artfully tied to furniture with brilliant red ribbon. Tall poinsettia plants spiked color where they were set atop tables. Christmas drawings from the children in his classroom hung from a long string of yarn by the banister.

Lieutenant Geary greeted them as they entered. "Welcome to my home, Mr. Huntington and Miss Dearing. Since this is Company C, Nineteenth Regiment of Infantry's last Christmas here, Captain Witherell has graciously given us leave to celebrate together."

Miss Dearing, attired in a splendid pink and cream skirt with a matching jacket, seemed to be blushing. "Thank you so much, Lieutenant Geary."

When Geary lifted Miss Dearing's hand to his lips, even the tiniest of Jesse's pupils could have knocked him over with a feather.

Miss Dearing and Lieutenant Geary?

Then their host, with Miss Dearing on his arm, led both classes into the parlor. Although spacious, the children spilled out into the hallway. Jesse remained behind in the kitchen, surveying the spread of desserts that Mrs. Christy had sent up from her shop. Fruitcake, scones, and numerous types of cookies covered almost every surface.

Moving into the kitchen entryway, Opal Duvall clutched her sister Bea's hand, eyes wide. "Is that awful Lieutenant Elliott here somewhere, teacher?"

The girls' beautiful sister, Sadie, had once been courted by the lieutenant. "He's on leave to visit his family, so no he's not here." Thank goodness, for the girls were still upset by the man's bad treatment of their beloved older sister. With their mother so ill, Jesse had not been sure the Duvalls would even attend the party.

"Good." Bea stamped her booted foot then swung Opal back around and headed down the hallway toward the parlor.

Jack Welling, dark rings under his eyes, shuffled into the kitchen with Ephraim. "We're ready for the decorating contest."

Jesse pointed to a pile of sugar cookies stacked on the oak counter alongside of three bowls of colored frosting and large shakers of various colored sprinkles. "I think those are what Miss Dearing wanted."

"We'll bring 'em to the dining room, sir." Normally, Jack would be off like a shot. His mother's pneumonia had worsened and instead the child ambled behind Ephraim, head bowed.

Whispering a prayer for both Mrs. Welling and Mrs. Duvall, Jesse turned in a slow half-circle to take in the spacious kitchen. Beyond the square space was a small room for a cook. But with only a dozen or so men left at the fort, Geary used the room as a study. He'd left a bowlful of walnuts atop his desk and several nutcrackers for the children to use later—for yet another contest. The older boys and girls would see who could crack the shells quickest.

Jesse stepped into the hallway that connected the kitchen to the study. A good-sized window to his right afforded a view of the roadway into the fort. Movement caught his eye. That was Maggie sitting atop the dray, stacked high with supplies. She was on her own today. His heart ached to think that soon she'd be leaving. But what could he do? He had nothing to offer her.

Captain Witherell's daughter, a notorious flirt who he'd been warned to avoid, sashayed into the small space. "Hello. I'm Dora Witherell, the captain's daughter."

Unease riffled through him as she smiled up at him in what most would consider a charming fashion.

"Jesse Huntington. Pleased to meet you."

A minxlike expression flittered over her even features.

123

Miss Dearing strode back into the kitchen, her pink-striped skirts swishing. With her blonde hair all piled in what his sisters called an 'updo,' she was indeed a pretty woman. "Mr. Huntington, the children are ready for the cookie contest."

He gave her a mock salute. "Yes, ma'am."

Miss Witherell flipped her palms opened. "Well, Miss Dearing has her lieutenant here but mine has not yet arrived."

His fellow teacher adjusted her lace collar. "Your father said he'd be here soon."

"Until then, may I borrow your associate, Miss Dearing?"

Borrow him? "It's only a few steps to the dining room, Miss Witherell." He gestured down the hallway.

With the tilt of her head, she reminded him of his mother and her expression when she was about to launch into full Southern Belle mode. "But with a handsome gentleman here to escort me, why would I want to be alone?"

Alone? She was in a house bustling with children. It was pointless to resist. Jesse extended his arm and walked the willful woman to the well-appointed dining room. Unfortunately, she didn't release his arm when he attempted to drop her hand.

Miss Witherell leaned in. "When Zebulon sees me with you, he'll think twice about being late the next time."

So she was hoping to make the lieutenant jealous. Jesse scowled. If it were Vivienne behaving in this manner, wouldn't he go along? Would it cause harm?

Jesse bent and whispered in her ear. "My dear Miss Witherell, I have two younger sisters. I'm not totally ignorant of the ways of young ladies. But I assure you, I'm also aware of how perturbed Lieutenant Vance would be to see me standing so close to you—especially since it's rumored he's to propose today."

124

"Propose?" Cheeks reddening, she blinked up at him.

He'd ruined the surprise, but by golly someone needed to wake this young lady out of her flirtations for a day which should be memorable for the right reasons.

"Excuse me." She whirled around and then strode off more quickly than he'd imagined her heavy skirts could possibly allow.

The children set about decorating their cookies, laughing and elbowing one another as they did so. Today, in contrast to earlier in the school year, the orphaned children were smiling and joking while Jack and the Duvall sisters kept to themselves, worry tugging at their features.

Private Abernathy, who'd ushered them in at the gate earlier, carried a mug of hot cider down the hallway. He stopped at the dining room and held the mug aloft. "Just bringing the dray driver something to warm him on his way back."

"I'll come with you. I'll bring Mickey something, too." He checked in with Miss Dearing and then grabbed a handful of cookies and wrapped them in a napkin. "Let me grab my coat."

He and Abernathy stepped out onto the broad porch. A cool gust of Straits of Mackinac breeze shot through him and he shivered.

Movement behind the Quartermaster's building, viewed in the space between that building and the adjacent one caught his attention. What were the men doing back there? And why was someone standing in the bed of the dray, with Maggie?

"Stop!" Someone's faint cry for help surged him into action. He raced down the wood walkway and then through the lightly snow-covered field toward the commotion.

Maggie had hinted to him that she believed the soldiers suspected she was a woman. He'd dismissed his niggling fears by rationalizing that the men wouldn't dare touch her with their superiors there as there would be grave consequences. No, that couldn't be it. They wouldn't. They couldn't do anything to harm the young woman who had come to mean so much to him. But as he neared the buildings he heard the Percherons sounds of distress. And then Sergeant Mauvais' distinct voice, "You're getting what's coming to you."

A knit cap and scarf, blue like the ones Mrs. Christy had given Maggie, flew out onto the snowy ground.

Jesse ran on, gaping as one of the privates climbed up into the dray and tugged at Maggie's overcoat.

Heart hammering, Jesse's vision blurred in his angry flight, but he couldn't miss as Sergeant Mauvais ran a finger under Maggie's chin and then bent and tried to kiss her. Quick as a flash, she wielded a horse whip up in her hand and brought it down hard on his head.

Jesse finally reached them, Abernathy on his heels, as the sergeant staggered backward but then lunged toward Maggie.

"Stop this at once!" Jesse rushed toward Maggie.

Knowing that he might be assaulted, he grabbed a thick branch from the ground in one hand and waved it at the men. "Don't make this any worse for yourselves."

Abernathy shook his head. "You'll face repercussions for your behavior today, Mauvais."

Sergeant Mauvais rubbed his head. "This little. . ." He let out a string of profanities. "She's been passin' herself off as a man for a long time and she needed to learn a lesson."

"I think you're the one who needs to learn a lesson, Sergeant." Jesse narrowed his eyes at the man, rushed at him, and commenced his instruction.

This would be a lesson that Mauvais wouldn't soon forget.

Epilogue

Pickford, Michigan April 1895

Maggie patted her shoulder-length curls in approval. "Thank you, Ma, for your help."

The woman in the mirror looked much different than "Mickey" had.

Ma pointed to Maggie's reflection in the oval mirror. "You do look right pretty."

Maggie swiveled around and took her mother's hands. "I don't think that's what caused Jesse to fall in love with me."

"I'd agree." Ma's face grew red.

"Have you been reading his letters?" Maggie searched her mother's face and found confirmation. "Ma!"

She crossed her arms. "Your pa snuck a peek, too."

Maggie gaped.

Her bedroom door opened, and her father ducked his head inside. "Look at my beautiful Hadley girls."

"I'm no longer a girl." Ma went to him and kissed his cheek.

Maggie raised her eyebrows. "And neither am I."

"At least you look like one, again." Pa made a swirly motion near his hair.

Maggie turned toward her vanity table and retrieved the pink crystal *vaporisateur* of French rosewater perfume that Vivienne had sent her. She sprayed the bulb several times. "Now I definitely smell like a lady, too. And not like a lady dray driver."

Ma laughed. "You're willing to give that up?"

"You've wanted to prove yourself for a long time, daughter." Pa's tone held a hint of secrecy. Or was he trying to make sure she'd be happy to be the wife of a Mackinac Island teacher?

Outside her window, a rider attired in a stylish coat, dark boots, and a top hat entered their yard atop a black gelding. Jesse. Her heart leapt.

"He's here." She pressed her hands to her mouth.

"We'll go greet him." Her parents left her, closing her bedroom door behind them.

Maggie's heartbeat skittered into a rhythm of its own. Ever since Jesse had rescued her from Sergeant Mauvais they'd been honest with each other about everything. He'd shared that he loved teaching too much to accept the offer from Florence's employer to move to Detroit. She'd told him of her desire, had she been a man, to run her own stable or dray business. And she'd confessed that she'd missed Hadley Farms so much that she sometimes felt ill on the island.

"Maggie?" Ma opened her door. "Someone's bursting to see you."

When Maggie entered the living room Jesse's eyes lit up. If he had opened his arms to her, she'd have swept into them—as she had after the attack. His arms were home, no matter where they lived. Tears pricked her eyes.

She loved him so much.

"I have news." Jesse's smile faltered.

"Have a seat." Pa gestured to their two facing divans by the fireplace. Jesse waited for Maggie to sit and then settled beside her at a respectable distance.

"Thank you Mr. Hadley for putting a word in for me with the Pickford School Board." Jesse brushed his dark hair back from his forehead.

Maggie felt her eyes widen. "Pickford Schools?" Jesse loved his island school.

"I have a contract offer." Jesse patted his pocket.

"Then Maggie and you would be nearby?" Ma clasped her hands together and beamed at Pa. But Maggie's father's eyebrows drew together.

"Maggie has some offers, too." Pa patted his own jacket pocket and then withdrew several envelopes.

"What?" Maggie reached for Jesse's hand.

"Let's hear them, sir." Jesse reached for and squeezed her fingers in reassurance.

"Mr. Stanley Danner, your sister Florence, and your mother all wrote." Pa dropped the opened letters down on the small oak table that sat between them.

"You opened my letters?" Again? At least if she were married she'd open her own correspondence.

"You'll find they're all addressed to me." Pa smirked. "With an additional unopened letter to you inside each one."

Jesse adjusted his eyeglasses. "Which leads me to believe you're somehow involved in these offers, sir."

"I did listen to and read all your business advice, young man, and perhaps I do have a stake in these offers. I do, after all, own a thriving Percheron business. And that's partly due to my daughter's sacrifice."

Her cheeks warmed at the praise. "I was happy to help." And she'd met Jesse doing so.

She retrieved the letters from the table and scanned Mr. Danner's first. "He'd like me to train his drivers either here in Pickford or on the island. Depending on where we end up living, he says." Maggie peered at Jesse, who hadn't officially asked her to marry him yet.

He opened the second one. "Mind if I look at Flo's?"

She waved her hand. "No, go ahead, everyone else seems to enjoy reading my mail."

Jesse chuckled as he read his sister's note. "Her employer asked Florence if there was something else she could do to help me, since I turned down the job in Detroit."

"And?" Maggie reached for the letter.

"Mrs. Schwartz bought the stables and dray businesses I suggested."

Maggie scanned to the bottom of the letter. "Florence says you and I could run the businesses together as they're all primarily in-season, when you won't be teaching."

"Oh, Maggie, we'd love to have you here but that's a dream for you." Ma's eyes filled with tears.

"Of course we'll expect you to enter agreements with Hadley Farms, upon suggestion from Mr. Huntington."

Jesse straightened his shoulders. "I had other good news from Florence recently. She's been collecting from Father's debtors. She's received enough already to begin repairs on our cottage—and for it to be winterized."

Maggie stared up at him. "That's wonderful news."

"Says it's her wedding gift to us." He shrugged. "I think she was just showing off for her boss, Mrs. Schwartz. And it worked because she's been promoted."

"Florence is such a great businesswoman."

"She is." Jesse frowned. "It's funny, because I overheard of a Mrs. Schwartz at the Wellings' home."

"Oh?"

"She sent a condolence card for Mrs. Wellings' death, but no one knew who the card was from. And then Grayson

Luce, Maude Welling's fiancé, said Mrs. Schwartz was his fraternity's house matron and a lovely lady."

"So no connection to Florence's employer though?"

"Common enough name. Sorry to digress."

She laughed. "It's all right. But what did Mrs. Huntington have to say?" The envelope to Pa was addressed from Atlanta, where Mrs. Huntington had gone after Christmas. Jesse's aunt had sent for her and faced with winter in the Huntingtons' small rental apartment over a store, his mother had quickly accepted.

Pa gave his head a tight shake.

"You read it, Jesse." Maggie sniffed and handed him the pale pink note.

He rolled his eyes. "If this says what I think it does, then she'll ask that you discuss her situation with me privately. She'd never put it in writing."

"Her situation?" Pa shifted in his seat.

"Ah, she's being courted by one of her old beaus and won't be leaving Atlanta until her own wedding date is firmly set." Jesse glanced at the note, waggling his head back and forth in impatience. "Yes, she wrote a note about nothing and I'm to tell you."

"But your sisters, they'll be able to come for a June wedding?" Ma leaned forward.

"Vivienne and her theatrical troupe will be returning to the island next week."

Jesse's youngest sister had been performing throughout the Midwest, despite Jesse's and his mother's objections. Vivienne simply left when Jesse moved into the apartment and sent him a telegram from Detroit.

"Russell will be happy she's back." Ma pressed her fingertips to her lips.

Pa cleared his throat. "Yes, they're quite good friends, I understand." His stern glance suggested that no one comment further on that topic.

Maggie stood and held her hands at her waist. "There seems to be a difficulty in making all these decisions, which assume I'm getting married."

"Oh, yes indeed." Jesse reached into his vest pocket and then dropped down on one knee. "It took being in desperate straits to open my eyes. If a lady dray driver will marry an island teacher, I believe God will bless us both."

Pa scratched his chin. "That sounds suspiciously like you're making up her mind for her. You take the Mackinac teaching contract, and she then helps run the island carriage businesses?"

Ma shoved Pa's arm. "You should know Maggie won't let anyone make up her mind for her."

"Yes." She laughed.

Jesse rose and embraced her.

When he released her, she schooled her face into a grave expression. "What makes you think I was agreeing to your *proposal* and not affirming my father's observation?"

"Because I'm a teacher and this year I've learned some lessons on love."

And she couldn't argue with that sentiment as he slid the ring onto her hand. "It's beautiful."

Pa took Ma's hand and led her from the room, affording Maggie some privacy with her new fiancé.

Maggie admired her gold engagement ring set with blue stones.

Jesse kissed her cheek. "Those sapphires in the ring remind me of Mackinac's waters out in the deep."

Maggie looked up at his beloved face. "If I'm going to be in desperate straits ever again—I want it to be with you. I don't know what I would have done without you."

"I feel the same. If I'm to be in desperate straits then I need to be with you." He bent and kissed her. And continued to kiss her until she became quite breathless.

When he pulled away, Jesse grinned. "Would a June wedding be too soon?"

She playfully swatted at him. "Your mother and sisters and my family need to make arrangements to attend. And our friends."

Ma popped her head around the corner of the room. "I've already reserved Pickford Community Church for the last Saturday in August."

"That way you and Jesse can get a honeymoon in before school starts." Pa playfully crinkled his nose as he barked out a laugh.

Maggie blinked at her interfering, but loving, parents.

"That's fine, Mr. and Mrs. Hadley." Jesse took her hand. "Maggie and I are going out to the barn visit Goldy and Silver."

"And Moo and Bear," Maggie added.

"Sure you are. I wasn't born yesterday." Pa pulled on his suspenders.

Jesse raised his eyebrows. "Please don't interrupt us out there, Mr. and Mrs. Hadley, as we'll be busy planning our wedding since you've scheduled it so soon."

Ma shook her finger. "I think you'll just be out there kissing, that's what I think."

Pa took her hand. "Let's leave 'em alone, Ma. We're done with our interfering."

"Until there are grandbabies." Ma raised her hand as if in pledge. "Then I get to start back up again."

Maggie laughed as Jesse pulled her toward the front door. Soon they were out in the barn, where the horses nickered in greeting.

As Ma had predicted, Jesse gave her a lingering kiss. When he stopped, he brushed her hair back from her brow.

"Did you ever think, when you met me two years ago, right here at your parents' farm, that we'd be engaged now?"

"Never. I thought I'd never see you again."

"And I never stopped thinking about the beautiful girl I met here—the one who could direct horses like a champion." He kissed her again.

She could stay in his arms all day.

Two nearby low neighs had them both laughing and they walked to the stables. Moo and Bear made snuffling noises. Farther down the row came two louder, more insistent neighs.

Jesse shook his head. "Goldy and Silver."

"Exactly. And they're ready to return to the island soon."

"I'm ready for everything to start happening. School lets out in a month."

"It'll be high season soon and a new beginning." Maggie squeezed the strong arms of the man who would become her husband.

"If God is for us then who can stand against us?"

"Let's keep trusting in God, not just in each other, to take us through all desperate straits we encounter."

"Agreed." And he kissed her, sealing their pact.

The End

Author's Notes

Did you know? Students in rural areas, especially in one room schools, were required to attend school from November through April and May until August, before 1900. My students in this novella are not needed for harvest. Instead, many of the island students and their families would have been busy the entire "high season" of summer. So for this story set in 1894, I have school begin in mid-September. There is an article on the www.heritageall.org site: Americas One-Room Schools of the 1890s. The Mackinac Island Public Schools at that time were housed in the beautiful Indian Dormitory. This was no tiny one room schoolhouse but a large imposing building not far from the fort. You can even visit this building today, which is part of the Mackinac State Parks.

In this novella I refer to the devastating Great Hinckley Fire, which really did occur in Minnesota in September 1894. My characters, however, are fictional.

Only a small number of soldiers lived at Fort Mackinac during this time. In fact, I had to stretch their occupation a bit for my story. As mentioned in Phil Porter's wonderful book, *A Desirable Station: Soldier Life at Fort Mackinac 1867-1895,* only eleven soldiers lived at the fort after 1892. I borrowed the real-life names of Captain Witherell, Lieutenant Geary, and Lieutenant Vance (used fictitiously) but the rest of the characters names and roles are fictional as are the captain's daughter and Miss Dearing (named for a special York High School teacher.)

There really is a large Percheron farm in Pickford, Michigan, in the eastern Upper Peninsula of Michigan, which supplies most of the dray horses on Mackinac Island today and for the past several decades. Owned by the Bishop family, Sweet Grass Farms Percherons is real—the Hadley Percheron Farm, however, is fictional. I've always loved Percherons. These gentle giants of horses do the hard work on Mackinac Island, which doesn't allow cars onto the island. So to visit, you must take a boat or ship and then travel by foot, carriage, horseback, or bicycle.

Part of the inspiration for this novel came during a hay wagon ride up to the Cannonball Express on Mackinac Island for barbecue. I was in an orthopedic boot for my foot (I could barely walk about five years) and I couldn't manage to get up onto the wagon bed. The wonderful driver, Judy Bishop, allowed me to sit up with her as she drove. She shared about her vocation with me. Years later, Judy became the manager of the stables. Fun fact—she manages the largest such enterprise in the world!

Thank you to my dear friend, my old Lake Superior State College roommate, Maggie Hadley Ribaudo, who let me use her name and those of her siblings in this story! Appreciation also to renowned horsewoman and writer Glenye Oakford and her husband author Christopher Oakford as well as their horse, "Moo", who leant their names to the story.

Abigail and Eli Mitchell are a real-life married couple who live in Virginia. Abigail is one of my long-time readers and I had the pleasure of meeting her and her husband in person. The stable helpers, Leonard and Jerry Zandi were named for my two cousins, now both residents of heaven.

Acknowledgements

To Abba Father – my hope is in You alone. Thank you to my son, Clark, for brainstorming a fun Victorian twist on the séance chapter. *Merci* to my amazing critique partner, Kathleen L. Maher for the original manuscript. Much appreciation to my Beta readers: Robin Auten, Susan Johnson, Rory Lemond, Sharon Robarts Kirby, and Nancy Judd Wagner as well as Advance Readers: Betti Mace, Rebecca Tellez, Heather Schmitz, Audrey Rolles and Joy O'Steen Ellis. God bless my Pagels Pals group members who support my writing ministry including vetting the cover for this novella. Thank you also to the Avid Readers of Christian Fiction group and to Martha Artyomenko, Administrator and author, for your support.

Thank you to Judy Bishop for inspiration for this story and for the kindnesses shown me both on that hay ride I took and for showing me around the Mackinac Island stables and answering my many questions! Judy is one amazing Yooper woman! Thank you also to Judy's sister-in-law, Erika Bishop of Sweet Grass Farms Percherons for all her help with my questions about the Percherons and their habits. Very much appreciated.

Thank you, too, dear reader for being a Christian fiction reader! Where would we authors be without our readers supporting our writing ministry? Many blessings to you!

Other Books in the
Mackinac Island Romances Series

Precursor to
Mackinac
Island Beacon

In Barbour's
Doors to the Past
Series

Mackinac Island Romances

My Heart Belongs on Mackinac Island
Maggie Award winner and a *Romantic Times* Top Pick.

Anchored at Mackinac
Gilded Age Romance on Mackinac Island

Mackinac Island Beacon
Mystery, double the romance, and women's fiction!

Associated books:
Behind Love's Wall (Barbour Publishing)

The Sugarplum Ladies – A novella associated with/prequel
to *Mackinac Island Beacon.*

The Substitute Bride – A novella

Dime Novel Suitor – A novella

Bio

CARRIE FANCETT PAGELS, Ph.D., is the multi-award-winning author of over twenty-five Christian fiction books, including ECPA and Amazon bestsellers. She loves a good cup of tea and keeps her teacart well stocked! The family dog, an Aussie Kelpie, walks her almost daily! Twenty-seven years as a psychologist didn't "cure" her overactive imagination! Carrie grew up in Michigan's beautiful Eastern Upper Peninsula. Although she now resides with her family in Virginia, she vacations most summers at the Straits of Mackinac—where many of her stories are set.

Social Media: Carrie is on Pinterest, Facebook, X, Instagram, LinkedIn, and more!

Website: www.carriefancettpagels.com

**If you enjoyed this novel,
a review is always
very much appreciated!**